Seeker Two
Voyages of the Seeker #2

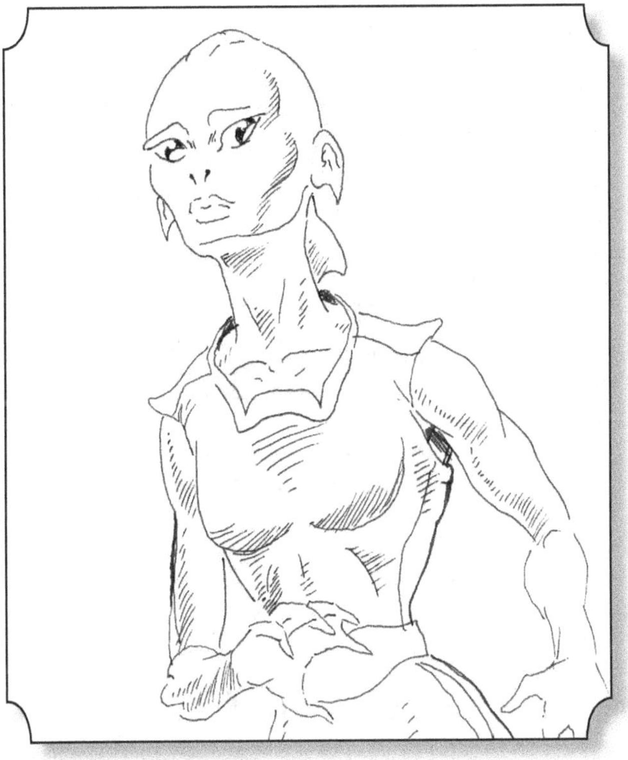

By Clint Hollingsworth

Illustration by Clint Hollingsworth

Published by Icicle Ridge Graphics. For permission requests, write to the publisher, addressed "Attention: Permissions Coordinator," at the website address below.

www.clinthollingsworth.com
Printed in the United States of America

ISBN-978-1-960216-02-1
Cover design by Clint Hollingsworth

Dedication

To Spirit and Opportunity.

"Good night, Oppy."

Chapter One

There is something absolutely magnificent about standing on the hull of a starship, looking at the endless wonders of our galaxy. I was staring outward at a colorful sky of nebulae, star fields, and distant galaxies and for a moment, I understood just how tiny and trivial I was in the grand scheme of an almost infinite universe.

If a person took a running start from a stationary object, in just the right trajectory, you could float forever. Not that you'd be there for most of it. The most advanced environmental suit wouldn't keep you alive long enough to even leave whatever system you were in. That alone would take multiple decades. Long past your expiration date.

These are things you can't help but contemplate if you have a few moments to stare out into the abyss.

I took a moment to take a look at our starship, the *E.S.S. Seeker*, now in orbit over the water-filled world we'd discovered. She'd been pretty badly battered before we'd started our repairs. Now, looking back toward the massive dorsal jump fin, the old girl looked almost normal except for some rippled hull plating.

"Cadet Voss," my radio blared with the voice of Chief Moreland. "We're out here to remove and recycle the damaged bits of the hull, not gaze at the stars or our new colony world."

"Aye, Chief," I replied. "It's just an amazing view, isn't it?"

"Yes." Moreland, usually the most acerbic of my superiors, let his voice soften for a moment. "Yes it is, and for once I don't blame you for goofing off, Cadet, but we have a ship to repair."

"Aye, Chief." I knelt down and resumed separating hull plate two-five-seven starboard from the the rest of the *E.S.S. Seeker*. Twenty minutes later, I was using a standard lever tool to float the plate upward and out to the awaiting arms and pincers of repair-bot K-45. Farther up the hull, I could see more of my fellow robotics section crew working on other rippled plating.

We'd all been co-opted from our maintenance duties as the ship's robotics staff to assume the grunt work of getting our vessel space-worthy again. Bot K-53 was already heading to my position with a new plate, fresh off the printer, to replace the section I'd just lifted out. Two of the ships main engineering personnel were approaching from the bow of the ship to oversee its installation, fourth-year cadets like myself evidently not being the first choice when actually putting the ship back together.

I moved twenty yards toward the bow. The front of our ship was well over a football field away but fortunately, this middle section was the only part that'd had much damage from a near miss in the battle we'd fought four months ago.

"Team three, this is Chief Moreland. Listen up. We're having trouble with some of the mining bots at the site on the outer moon. I'm heading out to see what I can do and I want to take our two junior-most members with me to gain field experience. Ensign Ping Teo, Cadet Tanner Voss, meet me in the belly shuttle bay in twenty minutes, and bring all your tools and a portable diagnostic kit. Everyone else, finish your shift here. Moreland out."

"Well. Sounds like fun, Tanner," a familiar voice said on my comm. A glance at my HUD told me it was coming in on a private channel. A very private channel.

"Where are you, Mom?" I said as I rounded up my magnetized tools.

"It depends," Dora, the AI who'd raised me as a child said. "Part of me is on Remora Two, trying to get surface scans of our new world here through some of the deepest oceans ever encountered. The other part of me is trying to help Doctor Thrace get access to the sealed parts of *The Beast*, and even though I am in overall control of this dreadnaught, I find that I don't have control over all the subsystems. It's a work-in-progress."

The dreadnaught she spoke of was the reason the Seeker was in need of so much repair. It was an alien artifact of unknown origin with a beam projector more powerful than any known weapon in the Laldoralin Hegemony. Fortunately for us, its computer systems were not more sophisticated than my Laldoralin-designed AI mom.

She'd literally saved all our butts by taking over the weapon/ship, which had done much to soften the anger of my captain at her having digitally stowed away aboard our Remora Two probe.

"Tanner, I can divert Remora Two to do overwatch while you and your team are on the outer moon and..."

"Mom, seriously... I didn't want you being overprotective a century and a half ago, when you were in faux-human form, long before my father put me in stasis. What makes you think I need to be coddled now? I'm a big boy, I don't need my mom watching me every second."

I had all my tools assembled, and in zero gravity they were easy to get in hatch Dorsal Five. I began stowing them in their lockers.

"There are concerns about the mining operation there, that you haven't been apprised of," she said. "The probable reason your robots there are having problems is the high degree of energetic particles coming from the Di-Kor-Van ore discovered there. That is why the Kiffalans have developed specialized ore-extracting machinery, specifically shielded, for mining operations on their own sixth planet."

"Has the captain been informed?"

"Captain Yamashita is fully informed on the subject," Dora said. "I am not sure that Chief Moreland is in the loop, however."

"Perhaps we should get him in that loop," I replied. "And honestly, considering my general standing with the Chief, maybe you should inform him of the particle problem."

"No, my son, I think I will let you tell him. A young man, even one who is half Laldoralin, needs challenges. Chief Moreland is one of your best challengers."

"Gee. Thanks."

◆

"You're sure on this? No one told me about high energy particles when we sent Minnie the Miner down there."

"Dora was the source, Chief," I told him.

"Well, that would have been good info to have before I packed this shuttle. Voss, Ensign Teo, unship and store those Mark I EVA suits and suit up in Mark II's. In the meantime, I think I'll have a little discussion with Science Officer Torvald about keeping his people who are actually doing the work, in the loop."

Ensign Ping Teo and I left the shuttle to return to the Robotics bay where we most often worked. Ping was a slender young woman of southern asian extraction and we both worked under Lt. Truval keeping our advanced sensor probes in good working order. Both of us, plus a few others, had been pulled out of that section to help with the ship repairs. This left a skeleton crew caring for all the various bots on the ship, as well as the Remora probes.

"Let's put the Mark I's in the suit locker in the shuttle bay, Tanner," Ping said. "We're gonna have a far enough distance to travel to get the Mark II's. Robotics bay is at the other end of the ship."

She wasn't wrong. The distance between the bays also meant we'd have to traverse a good portion of the ship, through some narrow corridors, in what amounted to two-legged tanks on the way back.

It took us about ten minutes to walk the length of the ship. We avoided some of the main corridors where repair work was still underway and at least twice someone tried to conscript us to work on their particular problems. Fortunately, our obligation to Chief Moreland kept us on track. The normally smooth, well-lit hallways were in various stages of disrepair and disassembly. Tools often needed to be maneuvered around. Engineers and crew-person techs were everywhere, from the huge hydroponics bay to the stellar-mapping hull extensions.

"Ensign?" I said. "I wonder, on the return trip, if it'd be faster to exit through one of the Remora bay hatches and walk the ship's hull to get to the shuttle bay?"

"I like the way you think, Cadet. Let's do it."

When we arrived at the almost-deserted Robotics bay, my mentor, Lt. Truval was waiting for us. "Moreland Chief has informed me of your new orders, young ones," he said. "I am preparing the Engineering Suits Mark II. One moment if you will please give me."

Truval, a sentient from the planet Botan, would best be described as sloth-like. The Botanans, being one of the long-standing members of the Laldoralin Hegemony, have a particular excellence in dealing with engineering, partly due to their having dual-purpose hands. Truval's hands had an over-set of fingers with large climbing claws, but under that, protected by the over-set, was a smaller set of twenty fine digits that make our opposable thumb design look 'quaint' in comparison. This enabled a mammalian race no larger than a big teddy bear to become the dominant species on a jungle planet with plenty of predators.

He had the suits checked and ready in about half the time a human could have done the same task.

"Sir," Ping said. "Cadet Voss and I would like permission to take the suits back to the Shuttle Bay One via the exterior hull, to avoid the congestion in the passageways under repair. I believe this will save us time and aggravation, if you agree."

"Yes," he replied. "I will prep the bay opening for Remora 3, young ones. Prepare for EVA once the door has opened and the pressure field is in place."

After a redundant systems check, and our individual Mark II's adjusting for our great variation in height, Ensign Teo and I were walking the length of the *E.S.S. Seeker*. We made much better time than we had on her interior. Not that Chief Moreland was going to give us any slack on that account. The Chief didn't actually have any slack in him.

Ping and I walked along the port side of the ship, passing the port extension lab, currently in its retracted state, the state used for traveling. Normally, this close to a planet, it would have extended thirty yards out into space, being accessed by the extension arm hallway. With all the repairs being done though, our captain had ordered all the ship extensions to be withdrawn into the *Seeker*.

Circling around and under the ship, we reached the largest shuttle bay, Shuttle Bay One. We entered the bay through the gravity shift hatch, which had a 90° turn to enable EVA personnel to switch gravity directions. Chief Moreland was standing by a Level Two shuttle in a Mark II suit with the faceplate up and the back hatch open. He climbed in the suit as we approached.

"Let's move, people. I would like to get this taken care of before the Captain decides we can stay behind on the Jump Drive test."

"I thought the people going down on the planet were just going to be civilian scientists and security people," Ping asked.

"Nope," Moreland replied. "Captain Yamashita has decided that part of the crew, likely the junior members and non-essential personnel, will also be going down to the landing site in case something catastrophic happens during the drive test. They've already enlarged the camp by thirty percent to accommodate everyone, as well as additional supplies and equipment drops."

"Oh," I said. "I don't like the sound of that. If you're saying 'junior members,' I'm probably gonna be one of those left behind."

"Maybe not," Ping said. "I've seen the basic plan for the test of the Jump Drive, and the *Seeker* will be deploying Remoras all along the jump track to maintain comms with the planet. Tanner, you and I are part of the Remora maintenance crew, so we might get to go along."

The three of us exited our Mark IIs, locking them in place, and took our seats.

"Seeker bridge, this is Chief Moreland in shuttle *LaStrange*, leaving main shuttle bay, enroute to moon S-2 for bot repair. Ensign Teo and Cadet Voss accompanying."

"Cleared for departure, *LaStrange*. Drive careful."

Chapter Two

The planet we'd discovered for Earth Colonization had been named, under the captain's prerogative, *Susanowo*. It was very Earth-like, with the subtle difference that 80% of the planet was underwater. Huge oceans so deep that even our highly advanced scanning equipment couldn't scan all the way down. Plenty there to still discover, but that job would likely fall to the colonists that would eventually follow us.

The planet had two moons, one of which could be habitable by humans with minimal terraforming and tweaking.

We weren't going to that moon.

Chief Moreland, Ensign Teo and I were going to moon #2, a sulphurous place with nothing resembling a breathable atmosphere. It also was a resource rich extravaganza, and was laden with certain charged metals that we could use in our replication printers. Everything we could scavenge to repair our starship was something we didn't have to deplete from our stores.

We hadn't named either moon, the captain having decided the future colonists should have the honors. The crew, however, named them unofficially Heaven and Hell. You can, of course, guess which one we were going to.

The Seeker was equipped not only with a jump drive, but also a primary drive that could go from tens of miles per hour to three times the speed of light. The Jump Drive would bring us to "Jump Space" and with proper calculations could send us vast distances throughout the galaxy. The primary drive (referred to as the FTL drive) moved us about locally.

Compared to both, our shuttle's Ion/Magnetic drive crawled like a dying inchworm.

Hell was almost exactly opposite of the Seeker's orbit, which meant we had to fly around the planet to get to it. It seemed to me it might've been better to wait until it came to us, which meant we could've been working on ship repairs while we waited. But I'm a Cadet, placed on the ship by an Admiral's whim and the request of a high mucky-muck father.

I'd learned when to keep my mouth shut, which was most of the time.

"Chief?" Ensign Teo asked. "You mind if I open the starboard-side ports? I like looking at the planet while I'm not having to keep track of hull plating."

"You're an officer, ensign, I'm an NCO. You don't need my permission. It's not like you're a crewman, or," he looked at me, "a cadet."

This seemingly snarky comment was still light years beyond how Chief Moreland had responded to my presence on the Seeker when I first came aboard. I had proven my worth against the alien dreadnaught Dora now controlled.

"Which units are on moon 2?" I asked. "All the small amount of info I've seen only states we have bot problems there. I assume it's Minnie-the-Miner we'll be working on."

"Minnie's there, but so are three floatbots, K-11, K-21, and K-6, who are supposed to be keeping things running, so us flesh-and-bloods don't have to spend a great deal of time in a corrosive atmosphere," Moreland replied. "K-6 had to get above the atmosphere to signal a need for assistance. Whatever the problem is, I'm guessing the designers of our mechanical friends seriously overestimated how much punishment they can actually take."

I pulled out my padd and began a quick review of systems for the huge mining machine. It was big enough that it had been ferried to the extraction location in three pieces and actually had a crew quarters and control room for use if the local robotic control was disabled.

Minnie actually took up a good portion of shuttle bay two, but her usefulness in extracting materials for our replication printers was what allowed the Seeker to be so far from home for so long. Much of the repair materials we were using to repair our vessel was coming from Susanowo's two moons.

Though I had specialized training in maintaining our Remora advanced AI probes the chief was making sure I was being trained in all the various robotic assistants we had on the ship. Hence the reason he'd brought me along on this mission.

"Have you worked on the big girl, Tanner?" Ping asked.

"On Minnie? I can't say that I have, Ensign. I've done a fair amount on the K-bots but I've only helped with exterior repairs on our miner."

"We'll see if we can change that, Cadet," the chief said over his shoulder. "But if it's really tricky, I may be sending you back in the shuttle to exchange for a larger, more experienced team from our robotics engineers. Nonetheless, I assure you, you will be more familiar with the big bot before this is done."

"I hope that won't happen. Aside from wanting to do new things, being sent back for lack of experience is embarrassing."

"No shame in not having experience, Cadet," he replied. "Only shame is in not striving for improvement."

The shuttle rounded the planet. Through the forward port, I could see the ochre-colored sphere that we'd named Hell. In the distance was the jungle moon Heaven. We looped around the former, coming to a location on the far side of the sulfurous moon. Chief Moreland dropped us toward the mining site and we touched down with barely a bump.

"Double check your Mark IIs before we exit the shuttle. I want to see all indicators green," he told us. When we'd all run a diagnostic with all indicators as they should be, we started moving into the airlock.

"All right, people," Moreland said. "We're on a moon in a completely different solar system, and just because we didn't see anything dangerous before, doesn't mean we're completely safe. Keep your eyes on your sensors and do regular full pulse scans every five minutes. Clear?" Ping and I both signaled assent. "Good. Now lets go see what's wrong with the babies."

◆

We'd landed around a hundred yards from the excavation site, but it was a short walk in the Mark II suits. Each suit is more than hyper-strong, shielded environmental armor: each suit is a computerized tool suite with everything from plasma cutters to a huge grouping of interchangeable assembly/disassembly tools. There isn't much an engineer can't take apart with what we have on our suits, or rebuild for that matter.

The previous tracks from the original deployment of the equipment were gone, blown away by the high velocity winds of Hell's turbulent atmosphere. However, it would take a very long time to erode the digging route Mini had left.

"There's our girl," Ping's voice stated over our comms. "Got her on the locator about 112 yards at 2 o'clock. She's dug a heck of a trench, chief. But wasn't she supposed to be excavating in a straight-line course?"

"Yes, the entire area here has the materials we need, so a straight course seemed most efficient," Chief Moreland replied.

"Then she's gone off course by a good margin," I noted. "According to my helmet comp, she should be about over there." I affixed a waypoint across all our helmet displays. "But the locator says she's off that by a good thirty degrees."

"What the...?" the chief said. "All right, lets see if we can find her. Ensign Teo, try to raise the floatbots. We need to interface with them to find out what the heck has happened to our miner's positioning system."

"I have them on my screen, Chief," she said. "But their power output levels look like they're offline. I'm only getting basic black box distress beacons."

"I see them on mine too. K-21 and K-6 are near where Minnie is signaling. K-11 seems to be over beyond that hill. Cadet, you make contact with K-11. The ensign and I will move on to the miner and see what we can see of our wayward AI friends."

"Aye aye, Chief. I'm on it," I replied.

"If K-11 is offline, extend your suit shielding and open him up for a re-start. Keep in touch."

"Will do."

"And Voss?" Chief Moreland said. "We can't be one hundred percent sure this is mechanical failure. Life here seems unlikely, but be alert. Anything's possible. Now get going."

I started trekking toward K-11's position. I was always a little careful around this particular floatbot, what with it having made a very strong effort to kill me once. Not that it was K-11's fault. It and many of the other floaters had been reprogrammed with a virus by an Earth for Earth saboteur who now resided in the *Seeker's* brig.

The Mark II suits cover ground very well, and the low gravity environment allowed me to make the trip using small jumps rather than trudging along. It didn't take long to reach K-11's position, and the bot lay there under a growing pile of drifted dust.

Its outer shell showed signs of light corrosion which told me that its magnetic shields were offline. A quick scan showed the bot's power levels at minimum, only enough to preserve its computer core. Kneeling down as best I could in my heavily armored suit, I reset my own mag-shield to wrap around the medicine ball-sized robot.

I extended a power/data jack from my wrist and, manually opening the small hatch on top of K-11, plugged in. Diagnostics confirmed my suspicions. The float-bot wasn't damaged per se, it had lost or had drained almost all its power. The loss of power must've happened very quickly. None of K-11's solar panels had deployed, not that they would've done much good in this murk. I began a trickle charge from my suit into K-11's system and checked in with my team.

"Chief? This is Voss. K-11 is almost completely powered down. I'm giving him enough charge to get him to the shuttle charging station."

"Get him b**ck… the shuttle…*** him in his charger, Voss." It seemed as they got closer to Minnie, the worse our reception was. "Teo and I are ***… to the miner bot and the other downed floatbots. Once you have K-11 in the shuttle, come join us."

"I wonder why K-11 was so far from his assigned area?"

"We'll find out when ***… have them all back online. Moreland out."

I took around ten minutes to get the bot charged up enough for its a-grav units to lift it from the ground. Another ten and I had the "groggy" bot ensconced in a charging bay. When we got back from whatever was going on at the mining bot, the floaters were going to have some explaining to do. Hopefully the fail-safe on their computer cores had protected their memories.

I exited the shuttle, and began the walk through the grainy, chemical-laden sand to the mining site. It was a short distance, but the heavy winds and dusty ochre-colored atmosphere made it hard to see what I was walking toward.

"This is Voss. K-11 is charging, and I am on my way to you."

"Tanner...Y**'ve got ... see this... Hurry," Ping Teo answered. Whatever it was they'd found, it was seriously degrading transmissions, and the transceivers on our Mark II's could easily reach a ship in orbit.

I picked up my pace, trying to ride the line between hurrying and losing my balance in the light gravity. Visibility was degrading even over the crappy conditions that had prevailed when we landed. I stumbled a few times, trying to hurry, but the Mark II's gyros kept me upright.

I finally found the trench the big mining bot had excavated, jumped down and took a hard right. I could see the vague outline of the machine. Moving toward the dark bulk, I realized that the large banks of lights intended to illuminate the area of the mining were either off or very dim. My face-plate heads-up display began ray-tracing shapes in green outline and informed me I was looking at the back of the mining robot.

Thanks. I think I got that.

A few seconds later, my HUD was outlined and identified my comrades. Chief Moreland and Ensign Teo were looking upward toward the front of the huge robot. Moving a bit closer, I saw why.

"What the heck is that?" I asked.

"Seems...sort... archw*y of... origin..." I heard bits of Ensign Teo's voice respond.

"I didn't copy that, can you repeat?"

Ping walked over and touched my arm with her gauntlet. "How's that, Tanner?"

"I copy. The suits conduct the signal better with actual contact?"

"Yes. We're using the suit's shielding as a method for verbal and data transfer," she told me. "As to what we've found, well it's a big archway, and Minnie is halfway through it. And the portion of her that's entered the arch has disappeared."

Chapter Three

Chief Moreland had decided this particular violation of the laws of physics was above our pay grade and returned to the shuttle to call in our science officers. I didn't blame him; though humanity had leapt centuries ahead in our tech, this was something completely new. He returned quickly, not wanting to leave two junior officers in charge of such a huge scientific find.

Looking at the arch that stood in front of us, I could see it was sentient-made. There were glyphs of some sort, several of which had a faint glow. The faceted arch was just small enough that Minnie's upper section had caught on it and preventing the mining bot from going all the way through. Somehow, the arch had pulled the big rig off its course and convinced it to try and enter the archway.

This however, wasn't the main scientific conundrum. Even though our miner was still powered and appeared to be functioning, her front half no longer seemed to exist.

"It looks like there's a cavern, or... something, beyond the archway," Ensign Teo said, "but I can't see any trace of Minnie's front end beyond it. This doesn't make sense. But at least this close to her, our comms are working."

"There's some sort of field generated right where Minnie disappears," I said. "Like a force field but I'm not getting anything off my suit's scanners." I reached out toward the field to see what it might do.

"VOSS!" Chief Moreland's suit gauntlet grabbed my own, "Do. Not. Touch! This is alien tech, for God's sake. We have no idea what it will do. What were you thinking?"

I was glad no one could see the embarrassed flush to my face through my helmet. "Sorry chief. That was a rookie mistake. I was..."

"You are a rookie, Cadet, never forget it. Now, do me the kindness of not shaving years off my life having to worry about what other "rookie mistake" you might make. Stand over there." He pointed to Minnie's rear section.

"Yes, Chief."

You know, if Minnie had actually been bisected, she wouldn't still have power," Ensign Teo said, pointedly ignoring my blatant faux pas.

"And look," I said, trying to put my mistake out of everyone's mind. "Her treads are still under tension. If she'd been cut in half wouldn't they be slack?"

"I suppose they would," the chief admitted. "It looks like… yeah. The miner's fusion reactor is right smack dab in the middle of the field our cadet so cavalierly tried to touch. Frankly, it should have detonated, with an explosion large enough to see from the moon's orbit. I think it's drawing power from Minnie, and somehow, her front half still exists. Somewhere. I hope Commander Torvald can solve this. Where the heck are the science kids anyway?"

As he said it, a second shuttle flew directly over us and a garbled transmission came from my speakers. "Morlan… we're …trouble…. position."

Chief Moreland sighed. "Voss, use your suit's scanners, track their descent and go bring the genius team back to us, while Ensign Teo and I keep an eye on things here. Go! Chop chop! Ping, you come with me."

"Yes, Chief," I said, setting out. The science team shuttle curved around to where our shuttle was parked and settled down next to it. I did my best to make good time to their location through the ankle-deep dust and sand.

The wind storm was starting to die down, and visibility was improving dramatically without the dust we'd been moving through all the time we'd been there. I could see the rear airlock opening, and two space suited figures emerged wearing Mark I suits.

We're not gonna want them to be out in this for very long with those Mark I suits.

While they were anonymous in their helmets, my H.U.D. designated both figures for me; Commander Torvald, the *Seeker's* head science officer, and Ensign Emily Darkfeather, his primary assistant.

"Cadet Voss reporting, Commander."

"Ah. Hello…th, …anner. I h…. you…. found…."The comm interference was worse out here farther from the artifact, which I didn't understand. It had degraded since we'd arrived. I reached over and touched Torvald's suit gauntlet.

"Can you read me okay now, sir?"

"Yes, clear as a bell."The commander motioned for Lt. Darkfeather to touch my other gauntlet. "Do you read us, Emily?"

"Yes sir. Good morning, Cadet."

"Good morning, Ensign," I replied, my heartbeat increasing. It was perhaps kind of ridiculous that she could have that effect on me through her EVA suit and my Mark II armor, but she did. Emily Darkfeather had once, in a moment of triumph related to our survival, grabbed me by the face and kissed me quite thoroughly. Being as this was a huge violation of shipboard regulations, me being several ranks below her, we were both very careful to never mention it again. Nonetheless, the attraction was pretty strong. At least on my end.

Wow, what a kiss. Unforgettable.

"Give us a quick rundown on what we've got going on here, Tanner,"Torvald said, jolting me back to here and now.

"Er.. yes Commander. We lost contact with the mining bot and when we arrived on this moon we found its three 'minder" K-bots all taken down from lack of power. Upon reaching the site of our excavator, we found the mining bot had been pulled off course and was wedged in an archway covered in writing unknown to the Laldoralin language database."

"Dammit. I should have brought Carstairs,"Torvald said, referring to our lead xeno-archeologist. "Well, lets have a look at this thing, then I can send one of you back to the *Seeker* to get her."

"Commander, there is one other thing. Minnie the Miner is in the archway, and we can see beyond the field that bisects the archway. It's a cavern of some sort, and beyond the force field, Minnie has… disappeared."

"It's front has been disintegrated?"

"We don't think so, sir. The field bisects her fusion reactor. Not only shouldn't there be any power, but Chief Moreland says the reactor should have explosively detonated. I noticed that her treads are still under tension. If the front half was destroyed, they'd be slack."

"Good eye, Cadet," Darkfeather said.

"Thank you, Ma'am."

"Commander," Darkfeather said. "This sounds like either the field across the archway is creating an illusion or perhaps… it might be some sort of portal technology?"

"Possible, though, as far as I know, none of the races of the entire Laldoralin Hegemony have been able to crack the nut of instant translocation. If you're right, Emily, this is a huge scientific find. Lets get going, I want to see this."

◆

"Wow. Just… wow." Commander Torvald said, staring at the glowing runes on the archway, as we all stood touching each other's gauntlets. "I definitely want more eyes on this."

"Sir," Darkfeather said, "My scanners indicate this archway has only been here between five to ten solar years. And yet, the material it's made of reads as over five hundred thousand years old. It's ancient beyond belief."

"How the heck does that work? The material has existed longer than almost all human or even proto-human technology. A lot longer. Hell, it might be older than our Laldoralin friends modern civilization." Torvald replied. "Ensign Teo?"

"Yes, commander?"

"I need for you to take one of the shuttles back to the Seeker and pick up Dr. Carstairs. I'd also like to bring Dora in on this for a Laldoralin perspective, so contact Remora Two and have her pop by if you would."

"Wait a minute, sir," Chief Moreland said. "Lets send the cadet, and keep the actual academy-completed engineer on site."

I heard the both Torvald and Darkfeather's chuckle over the comm and prepared for humiliation. Sometimes it was NOT good to be the cadet.

"The captain has asked me to oversee the training regimen that Chief Kurakin has been putting our young cadet here through via the various section chiefs," Torvald replied. "Needless to say his gunnery scores are off the charts, and he's doing well in all his subjects except one."

"Let me guess," Moreland responded. "Flight and helm. Piloting."

"Yup. Lt. Kolara has approved him for some of the smaller shuttles, but our large cargo shuttle seems to evade him. I believe in one of the sims, he managed to take out an entire shuttle bay."

"Dammit, Voss!" Moreland said. "Why the hell do I have you out here? I should have sent you to play in the simulators and brought Shendra out here with us."

"Yes Chief." What else can you say in such a red-faced situation? "I'll try to do better. I actually did pretty good on the sims where I was helming the *Seeker*, it's just the smaller craft…"

"That doesn't do us much good at the moment, Voss. Ensign Teo, do as the Commander says."

"Roger that, Chief. On my way, Commander." Ping started toward the shuttles. At that moment, I wished I was going with her, but turning back toward the archway I changed my mind. I wanted to know what the heck was going on here.

"Out of curiosity, Chief, has anyone tried to access the cabin controls? It looks to me like the human quarters and control area are still on this side of the… whatever it is." Torvald asked.

"Not yet," Chief Moreland replied. "We wanted the big brains to take a look before we touched anything. We can access through the rear hatch. Maybe Minnie's readouts can give us a clue as to what's going on."

"All right," Torvald said, taking a last look toward the arch. "Let's open her up and see what we can find out."

Chapter Four

Standing on the side track cover of a huge robot/miner/shuttle, trying to reroute a power conduit is a difficult job aboard the Seeker in regular coveralls.

Trying to do it in an armored Mark II engineering suit, in low visibility/gravity with an alien artifact looming overhead is a bit nerve wracking. Combine all that with my not having worked on Minnie that much, and I was listening very carefully to Chief Moreland's instructions. He was standing on the opposite side of the miner mirroring my position.

"All right, Cadet," His voice said over my helmet's speakers, "this might seem a little daunting, but it's gonna go smooth as butter. I will go through the process on my side and describe the whole thing in stages. You will follow along, doing what I say and we'll then see if Commander Torvald's idea of re-routing power from the secondary drive train will enable us back her out from… wherever her front end has gone."

Following along with the chief, we rerouted the power feeds a section at a time. I clicked over the last relay just after he did and told the chief we were golden.

"Commander, we've got the shunts done. See if you can get her to back out."

"Roger that," said Torvald. "Brace yourselves."

"Greetings Commander," a new voice spoke over the transmitters. "Remora Two now on station. Might I suggest that you hold off on what you are attempting until I can finish a scan set of the artifact?"

"Ah, Dora the Remora. Glad to have your help. Initiate your scanning and we'll sit tight."

Looking up, I could see Remora Two, AKA my mom, floating about thirty meters above the surface of the minerbot. I knew she could see me and no one else could, so I gave her a wave. A few seconds later, her starboard and port running lights alternately blinked, her probe-body method of waving.

"Commander Torvald," Dora said. "I am reading exotic particles moving in mobius patterns around the area. It also appears the edifice itself is not actually a solid but is some form of nano-technology, possibly malleable. The particle waves are quite similar to experiments the Kiffallans tried several centuries ago in the pursuit of instantaneous trans-location."

"Since the jump technology the Hegemony shared with us is far from instantaneous," Torvald replied, "I assume that line of scientific inquiry went nowhere?"

"Molecular degradation was the unfortunate result of the experiment. Any item sent through that matrix crumbled after the second attempt. Needless to say, no trials on living beings were ever attempted."

"I should think not," Torvald said. "So, do your scans indicate there's any trouble with us trying get this artifact to give us our miner back?"

"For God's sake, wait!" A new voice came over the comms.

"Carstairs? Is that you?" Torvald asked.

"Yes, the shuttle is almost there. Before you do anything, let me see the artifact. Maybe I can tell you if there's any kind of warning on it."

"Roger that, Doctor. We're reading you five by five. Dora, are you enhancing our communications?"

"Affirmative, Commander. I have compensated for the interference from the artifacts particle waves. I am keeping a minute by minute upload to each of the other remoras as well as my twin-self on the Beast," She replied. "Just in case."

"Just in case?"

"Just in case the unknown gets feisty."

◆

It was only a ten-minute wait before Dr. Carstairs, our resident civilian xeno-archeologist, made it from the shuttle to the dig site.

The winds had died down, and she followed our tracks without difficulty. I hadn't ever had occasion to interact with her, though I'd seen her. It was going to be interesting to see what a xeno-archeologist was going to make of our discovery.

"Mother of…" Carstairs said. The doctor was a short woman, red-headed and thin as a rail. Even with her EVA suit on, she seemed tiny. "Dora, you said you thought this was some sort of portal?"

"Yes, Doctor. With what we see here, the front end of the mining bot is not there, disappearing about midway though its fusion reactor. It should have been destroyed. As it seems to be working within acceptable parameters, we conclude that the front half of it must exist somewhere else while still being part of the whole."

We watched the archeologist wander around the front of the portal, taking scans and photos of everything. It seemed to me that time was of the essence here, and Carstairs was wasting time taking photos and scans, inferior scans, of what Dora had already taken. Did Carstairs not know this? Or was she wasting time on purpose? I'm just a lowly cadet so I couldn't correct Dr. Carstairs' scientific methodology.

"Dora," Dr Carstairs said, "These glowing runes. Is there anything in the Laldoralin databases that is similar? These look almost Medegin in their flowing nature. Maybe the originators were aquatic or amphibian?"

"There are similarities. Constructing a translation matrix of this resemblance would be problematic without much more data."

"Doctor Carstairs, can we try backing Minnie out now?" Chief Moreland asked.

"Minnie?"

"Minnie the Miner. Her nickname."

"How quaint," Carstairs replied. "I think you can go ahead. I'd very much like to see the entire edifice without a large robot stuck in it."

A private channel opened up on the corner my HUD with Emily Darkfeather's face showing in it. "Looks like someone just found their research publishing efforts for the next decade or so."

"Yeah," I said, laughing. The software in my helmet knew to cut my connection to the group comms when a private channel was employed. "I hope she knows that when the Seeker moves on to the next world in our possible colony survey, she won't be able to stay. She'll have to hand it off."

"We'll see. Torvald is talking. Looks like we're up."

We both switched channels back to main comms. Torvald's last words were on the side of my HUD as text.

"All right. Chief, let's get you and Tanner back up to your positions and Darkfeather and I will see if we can get our wayward bot to back out of there."

◆

Back on the track cover, I watched the shunt I'd set like a hawk. In a situation like this, there was a tendency for the energy flow to try to return to its regular flow path. Not on my watch.

I could feel the rumbling of the miner as Commander Torvald tried to reverse its course. When you can feel that much movement through a Mark II suit, you know a lot of power is being employed. Looking down, I could see the dust begin to move away from the gate, as if a wind was blowing it, a wind that blew outward in all directions in a perfect circle.

"Commander," Dora said, "I'm seeing the particle streams surrounding the edifice accelerating. As you draw more energy from the miner's fusion reactor, the faster they're moving. It appears the artifact is drawing more power from you the more you increase the reactor's output."

"Keep me posted," Torvald replied. "If anything looks dangerous, I'll back off the throttle. Dr. Carstairs, do you read me."

"I'm here."

"Please come to the back of the miner bot and join us inside. Ensign Teo, Chief Moreland and Cadet Voss are in those tank-like

Mark II suits. Your Mark I is much less robust so I think it'd be better if you were in here with Darkfeather and I."

"Understood, Commander. I'm coming in now."

"Chief? I'm about to max out our power. If this won't get her free, I don't know what we're going to do."

"Understood, sir. Teo? Back up Voss on that starboard power shunt."

"Roger that, Chief."

In other words, keep an eye on the cadet.

It was a little tight having two people in the big engineering suits working at one spot, but at least the chief hadn't asked her to take over for me. I'd had enough humiliations for one morning.

I could feel the vibrations through my suit ramp up even further and felt a vague push from the direction of the arch. I glanced down toward the treads.

"Ping! Look down there. The magnetic resonance is pushing the dust away from the arch in a perfect arc."

"Yeah," she replied, looking down at the moving dust. "But what's that being exposed under it. It looks like… no… can't be. Dora? Can you scan the substrate the miner is sitting on? The dust is clearing away."

"Scanning," Dora said. "Oh. Oh dear."

"Are those what I think they are?"

"Yes ensign. You are looking at a mass of crushed bones. Unknown species, but with DNA markers similar to our Medegin allies." Dora replied. "The sheer amount of mass and the sizing of the bone structures indicates many, many thousand individuals. You are essentially standing on a grave…**"

Dora's voice cut out instantly. I felt a wave of vertigo wash over me as it happened, then I was seeing stars.

"The Arch! It's changing shape!" I heard Chief Moreland over my comm. It's growing larger! I…I…"

I felt as if I was turning into living powder. Time seemed to slow. I raised my gauntlet in front of my faceplate and my arm was composed of glowing motes, flying off me and toward the gate.

"What's..." Ping's voice came over comms, "happening... to..."

I felt my consciousness slipping away. Slipping into the gate.

Chapter Five

Black desert?

Slowly I climbed my way out of the pit of unconsciousness, my whole body tingling like I'd been shocked. Before me, through my helmet's faceplate I could see black granules.

Burnt matter? Was I disintegrated?

Then why do I still have thoughts? Could I have thoughts without my body?

No, that didn't make sense. I noticed something dimly flashing on the side of my vision and moved my head to see what it was.

It was an icon. An icon of an old time battery and above it, an dimly lit icon that showed a stylized sun.

I know what that means, if only my brain would work.

The clouds in my mind eventually parted and I remembered I was in the Mark II suit. The icons were trying to tell me something. The flashing battery sign meant that my suit was very low on power. The flashing sun meant the suit had auto-deployed all of its solar collection surfaces.

Not good.

I tried to move to a sitting position, but had no luck. Evidently the power core in my suit had gone below the threshold for regeneration of power, which was why the solar collectors had auto-deployed. I just hoped I was in some sort of sunlight, preferably unobstructed or I'd be here a while.

I'm laying on a surface. Gravity, feels like full gravity, is affecting me, I'm not in space. Do not panic. Call for help.

"This is Voss. Does anyone hear me?"

A vague buzzing, that could've been a transmission, came over the RT. If everyone else, assuming they were alive, was in the same difficulty as myself, they probably didn't have much power to transmit.

More waiting.

As I watched, a small indicator bar appeared telling me I was at nineteen percent power.

I am recharging. Must be in sunlight! Just a bit more and...

A humming started at the small of my back, and all my power indicators began to climb rapidly. The solar surfaces, with their Laldoralin advanced particle attraction technology, had brought in a enough energy to achieve restart for the tiny reactor powering the suit.

Back in business! Oh thank God!

I sat up, back granules falling away from my faceplate, and realized they were some sort of sand. My visor took a moment to polarize from the bright sunlight suddenly hitting it and I got a good look at my surroundings. I'd been laying in a small patch of black sand surrounded by low-lying vegetation. The flora nearby consisted of what appeared to be blueish-green grass intermixed with purple succulents that reminded me of Purslane back on Earth.

"What the hey? This almost looks like..."

"Warning. This is an automated distress beacon from Remora Two Probe, serving *E.S.S. Seeker*. Any Terran Exploratory Force personnel in the vicinity, this probe needs assistance. Power levels are critical and data loss may ensue if assistance is not rendered."

"Mom!" I lumbered to my feet and wheeled around, looking for her probe body. Instead, I saw Ensign Teo slowly getting to her feet, her power armor evidently now on line. "Ping! Have you seen Dora?"

She pointed behind me, and began moving in that direction. Getting my suit turned around, I saw Remora 2 at the end of a shallow trench, the unit lying on its side.

"Hang on, Dora," Ping's voice came over the RT. "Auntie Ping's gonna get your power core restarted."

Shit! Did she lose so much power her intelligence was damaged?

As I stood there, worried, Ping detached a power cord from her wrist control section and manually opening a hatch on Dora's port side, jacked in. A few seconds later, solar collectors began to appear all over Remora 2's surface. The few exterior lights on her module began to glow brighter.

It may be weird to worry about an artificial intelligence this much, but Dora was the only mom I'd ever had. I hadn't even known she was artificial when I was young and she was in an android body. She was just my normal 'human' mother.

"Mom? You in there?"

"Yes, Tanner. Thank you, Ensign Teo. I pulled all the remaining power from this module to try and preserve my program integrity. Give me a few minutes and I will be operational again. I appreciate the save."

"My pleasure, Dora. Tanner, please go check on the Chief and then we need to ascertain the miner module's status. Once Dora's up and running again, maybe she can tell us where we are."

"Aye ensign." I looked around, and finally noticed that Minnie was indeed with us, just a few yards from the gate. A different gate. The terrain around it looked familiar. "From what I can see, though it looks like we're down on Susanowo. Down on the planet we were orbiting."

"Look like it to me, also," Ping replied, "but let's not take anything for granted. Go find the chief."

I started out at a trot, or the best approximation one can get while in an eleven-hundred pound suit. Looking behind the bot, the portal, definitely looked different. The shape was different, and the runes seemed to be in different places. Minnie the miner was about twenty yards out from its entrance. She was all there.

As I rounded the silent miner bot, I saw Chief Moreland lying face down in his suit, but what I didn't see was the exposed solar collector surfaces exposed. His suit wasn't recharging.

"Ping," I said through my suit's comm, "the chief's suit isn't recharging, I'm going to jack in and see if I can feed him power."

"Oh, I hope it's that his suit was drained more than ours were, rather than a major malfunction. Keep me in the loop."

I manually opened the power port cover, and jacked in to feed the chief power from my generator. The indicator on the port didn't move. My helmet told me no energy was being transferred, not good.

"Ping, his suit won't take power!"

"I'll be right there. Dora has enough juice to recharge herself. I'm on my way."

"I think his suit's malfunctioned. We may have to crack it open," I said, doing my best to keep panic out of my voice. With no life support, the chief might be out of air. I had no idea how long we'd all lain there.

"I hope there are no serious bugs here, then," Ping replied.

"If it's Susanowo, then we're inoculated. If not, running out of air will kill him a lot faster than any bug." I began undoing the bolts that would manually open the back of the chief's suit. A few moments later, Ensign Teo joined me and we quickly popped the back hatch of the engineering suit open. A very sweaty-looking Chief Moreland greeted us with a gasp and several deep breaths.

"Damn!," he said, sitting on the edge of his hatch in the bright sunshine. "That was getting dicey. I was about to pass out."

"I couldn't get your suit to take power, Chief," I told him.

"Yeah. I got that. Have you two checked on the folks in the miner, yet?" He said as he climbed out of his inert armor.

"That's negative, chief," Ping said. "You get your breath, and Tanner and I'll go check on them." He waved us on, while he gulped more air. Ensign Teo and I lumbered over to the back of our miner craft/robot and she opened the manual panel.

"Some of Minnie's indicator lights are still lit, but they're dim,' she said. "Tanner, lets see if we can open her electronically before we start pulling manual releases. Jack in on your side, and I'll do the same over here. Maybe we can boost the power just enough to get the hatch to open like it's supposed to. What's the power level on your suit?"

"I'm back up to seventy-three percent."

"I'm at six-seven. Let's do this."

Jacked in to Minnie the Miner's ports, we trickle-charged the door and in a few moments it responded to our commands to open up. Looking in, I could see Commander Torvald, Lt. DarkFeather and Dr. Carstairs. They all looked okay and eager to come out in the sunlight.

"Good to see you two," Torvald said. "Minnie's power core is off-line again. Looks like she needs a jump-start."

"Once our suits are back to full charge, sir, we'll see if we and Dora can feed the old girl enough juice to achieve restart," Ping said. "Chief Moreland's suit malfunctioned, and we had to remove him manually. He's sitting out exposed to wherever we are."

"Hoo boy. Obviously we're not on Hell anymore. Hopefully it's not a disease-ridden place. We've been blind in there. Any idea where we wound up?"

"Commander, it really appears to be Susanowo, as far as we can tell," I said.

"We don't know that for sure," Ping said. "We're going on visual cues with no scan data yet. Dora's only now coming on line, Sir."

"Have you attempted to contact *Seeker?*"

"Er.. negative, Commander. We only got our Mark II suits up and running a few minutes ago," Ping told him.

"Tanner?" Torvald said. "Get a little bit away from the archway and punch a call up to them. Your Mark II should have enough power for that now. Check in with the Seeker and update them on our situation down here. Then go check on Dora."

"Affirmative. I'm on it."

I moved fifty feet away from Minnie and using my HUD interface I sent a signal into space. "*Seeker*, this is Cadet Voss. Do you copy?"

Nothing.

Looking at my indicators, there was no comm chatter on our usual frequency at all. Nor on any of the associate bands in the same range. Even if there was atmospheric distortion or severe solar activities I should've been able to pick up something even if it was too distorted to understand. Also, we had teams on the surface of the planet. I should at least have been able to touch base with them.

"This is Cadet Voss. Can any T.E.F. personnel listening please chime in. My team and I are on the planet through some sort of gateway tech. We need assistance."

Again, nothing.

I switched to a side frequency used to stay in touch with the Remora probes. "Mom? You got your ears on?"

"Metaphorically, yes, Tanner. I monitored your attempt to contact the *Seeker* and in a few moments I will be up to strength enough to begin using my scanning suite. I can tell you right now, I am finding nothing on any frequency that the T.E.F. or for that matter, the Laldoralin Hegemony uses. There are transmissions on a lower band though, and they are not naturally occurring."

"What? But as far as we could tell, we had no intelligent life here on Susanowo."

"Assuming that's where we are," Dora replied. "Nonetheless, these signals could not have come about through random radio waves."

"Then, it would seem, we're not alone down here and that we have new players on the field," I said. "We better tell the commander. How long until you're up to full power?"

"I estimate an approximate time of ten minutes, allowing for differing power access input. Even without my full scanning suite activated, I am able to read intense solar surges in the upper atmosphere."

"Y'know, Mom, I'm looking off to the south, and I'm almost sure I see traces of the nebula we've been looking at for the last month through this sunny sky,' I said. "I'm also almost sure this is Susanowo, but the star was very stable the whole time we've been here. Why is there so much activity now? It can't have been more than a short time since we were pulled here. There's no way, even moving at light speed, that solar flare energy could've made it this far in such a short time, is there?"

"Since solar flare radiation moves at the speed of light, it could have arrived here in minutes. However, such radiation would not go from 'no indication' to 'all-out radiation burst' that quickly. From the power levels in my core degradation, and my monitoring them as they decayed, I do not compute that we were placed here anymore than an hour and twenty-minutes before you came to my rescue."

"This seems like an issue for the science team," I said. "Hopefully Commander Torvald and Ensign Darkfeather can shed light on this conundrum."

Chapter Six

"And as soon as Mom… er.. Remora 2 is at full strength, she can tell us if this truly is *Susanowo* or not." I said.

"All indications seem to say it is," Commander Torvald replied, "Some of this flora around us is definitely similar to what we encountered in the initial botanical studies. But it pays to have actual stellar data before jumping to a conclusion."

"Dora? You ready to rock yet?" Emily Darkfeather asked.

There was a moment's pause then Remora 2's channel opened. "I am now at 100% power. Commander, request permission to go to high orbit for my scanning session."

"You are green for orbit, Remora 2," Torvald said. "Let us know what you find as soon as you can."

"Affirmative."

We watched as the probe my mom lived in rose up and headed for orbit at a high rate of speed. Within moments she was lost from sight.

"While she goes and does her thing, troops, lets see if we can help Chief Moreland get the solar collectors on Minnie engaged."

"Is the chief's suit operational yet?" I asked.

"No," Darkfeather replied. "Ensign Teo fed him power while you were gone, and the solar rechargers wouldn't engage. Nor could she feed him power to try and restart the suit's own mini-reactor. Seems the entire Mark II has malfunctioned. Lucky for him there's an atmosphere here." The rest of us were still breathing suit air.

"We'll worry about my suit when this mining bot is charging up," Chief Moreland's voice came from above us. I could see where he'd climbed to the top of Minnie through the upper edge of my faceplate, manually opening solar recharger hatches. "Probably something easy to repair, but priority one is getting this big girl back on line. Her transceivers are far better than anything we can put in a single power suit. She is also a good first line of defense if we're not where we think we are."

"Do you think there might be danger, chief?" Dr. Carstairs emerged from the mining robot's cab.

"There can always be danger, Doctor. There's less danger if you prepare for danger."

I looked around. The scene seemed idyllic. In the distance, beyond what appeared to be trees, I could see a vast ocean shimmering in the bright sunlight. The sky was a deep blue with faint aurora streaks flashing thought it. In the sky, I could see one moon that looked a lot like the one we'd nicknamed Heaven.

I hoped the chief was just being paranoid.

"Maybe the chief has a point," Torvald said. "Ensign Teo, walk a mile or so at eleven o'clock from Minnie. Cadet, you accompany her. Keep a fix on us here, and let us know what you see. A little immediate vicinity recon might be in order."

"Yes, commander," Ping and I said simultaneously.

I turned from the group and began to maneuver my suit overland in the direction indicated. Ping walked beside me.

"Tanner, switch to channel 4, would you?"

"Sure Ensign," I said. Switching channels would basically give us the ability to talk privately. "Can you hear me?"

"Copy. So. The theory seems that we are on *Susanowo*, but there are so many differences."

"Such as?"

"The sky is different," Ping said. "It looks similar, but that nebula in the southern sky is smaller than the one we were seeing on planetary missions. I'm sure of it. And *Susanowo* had a lot more trees. There are trees here, but they're in clumps, as if they were left alone in certain places and... I dunno... removed everywhere else."

"I'd have to take your word for it. I only made it down to Susanowo's surface twice, you know, being a cadet and all. Also, a planet is a big place. Think of how many different bio-regions there are on Earth."

"Yeah. Hey, can I ask you about that? Being a cadet on this mission?"

Oh boy. Here it comes.

"I suppose," I said. "To preemptively answer, yes. My Laldoralin high-mucky-muck father did want me on this mission. The admiralty concurred because of some special talents I and my sister, who's serving on the Wanderer, both have. Yes, I grew up with a pair of Laldoralin AIs in android bodies as my parents. No, I didn't know they were AIs until just before this mission. Yes, my sister and I were in cryo for about a hundred and fifty years, so we were born in the 21st century. Does that about cover it?"

"All very interesting, and I will want to hear more on all of that, especially what the 21st century was like," she said. "Actually, I heard through the grapevine that somehow you are the reason that we're all still breathing. How's that work?"

I hesitated to answer. It hadn't been ordered by Captain Yamashita, but it had been implied that I should keep my special talents to myself. Having been looked upon as both a savant and a freak at different times, I tended to do that naturally.

Ping sensed my hesitance. "C'mon, Tanner. If my theory is right and we're not on *Susanowo*, then it may be a long time, if ever, before we're back to our ship. It won't hurt to satisfy my curiosity."

She had a point, though I wasn't willing to concede that things were worst case yet. We still couldn't be sure with such a cursory reconnaissance that we weren't on our familiar planet.

The honest truth for me was that I was tired of members of the crew thinking I was only placed on the ship because my "father" (and I use the term loosely) pulled strings.

"Can you keep this to yourself, Ping?" I asked. "It was implied that I shouldn't be blabbing about what happened."

She made the classic 'zip your lips' hand signal, which looked kinda silly over a polarized faceplate. "I can keep a secret, Tanner."

"Okay. The main reason I was placed on *Seeker* a year before graduating the academy, is that my sister Valiel and I both have a talent which seems to come from the fact that she and I are human/Laldoralin hybrids. It's kind of an extra-sensory perception."

"Like telepathy?"

"Ehhhh… kinda sorta. Val and I can't communicate like that, it's more of a knowledge of danger. When we were fighting the *Beast*, the captain gave me permission to advise the helm officer when to dodge. I knew when the big hits were coming and until the last, we were able to keep away from that big particle beam."

"Holy… is that all of it? Or is there more?" Ping asked.

"The other side of the talent is my being able to know where to hit my opponent. You know there were two attack modules on the Beast that separated to make a three pronged attack, right?"

"Yeah. We destroyed one and heavily damaged the second. Not bad for an exploratory vessel."

"I was at tactical," I told her. "We weren't getting through their shielding before I was put there. I knew instinctively where to shoot, how to shoot, and when to shoot. So, as I said, it's some form of extra sensory perception. I've had it since I was a kid, before Krizon put Val and I in suspended animation. Val has it too. No other Laldoralin hybrid from any of the other races seems to have it."

"Not Shendra or Duala?" She referred to our second engineer on the *Seeker*, and her sister working in the med bay.

"They've told me they have some telepathy, but only between the two of them. Nothing like this."

"So does this work in space and say… like down here?"

"Seems to. At the academy, I was skunking my fellow cadets in tactical sims, until I realized that made me stand out like a sore thumb."

"Wow. Well it may come in handy wherever we are…" She noticed I'd stopped.

"Hey Ping?"

"Yes?"

"Your theory that we're not on *Susanowo* may be right. Look there," I pointed. "And set your visor to 3x magnification."

She swiveled her Mark II toward me, and even through her helmet, I could tell the moment she enlarged the view.

"W-what? Is that what I think it is?" She said.

"If you think you see a gleaming city beside the sea, then, yeah."

"Oh Toto, we are not on *Susanowo* any more."

Chapter Seven

"We are definitely on *Susanowo*."

"But Dora," Commander Torvald said. "Ensign Teo here has reported seeing a large urban area less than twenty miles to our northwest. Now, I have looked at a lot of our survey scans on *Seeker*, and I'm quite confident I wouldn't have missed that."

"You are correct. However, that applies to the time that we were in previously."

Dead silence. The commander finally looked at Mom's optical sensors with a stunned expression on his face. "Dora? Are you telling me that we are not in the same time period we were in this morning.? That we've somehow traveled... through time, itself?"

"Affirmative. My recent cursory scans of this world indicate a fairly high level of civilization, with multiple large cities across several of the archipelagos. My deep stellar scans indicate the stars are not positioned in in the proper place to be the time period *Seeker* exists in."

Dora paused a moment to let that sink in.

"Then," Dr. Carstairs asked. "Are we in the future? Are those human colony cities?"

"And why does the nebula look different?" I asked, gesturing at the large stellar phenomena to the south. It was much more prominent in the twilight sky than it had been in full daylight.

"To answer both questions, we are in what would be, to our orientation, the past. As best I can calculate, we are five hundred seventy three thousand, three hundred and forty-two Earth years before the date the *Seeker* entered this star system, plus-minus two years. The nebula has not yet assumed the particular shape that we are familiar with. The cities in question? It is highly unlikely that humans had anything to do with them."

I realized I was breathing fast, and my heart was racing. Looking around at the gobsmacked look on everyone else's faces through their helmets, I wasn't the only one.

Dr. Carstairs broke the silence. "The portal. We have to use the portal to get back home!"

"I'd like to hope that's possible," Ensign Darkfeather told her. "But we got here on a fluke. We're going to have to take time to study what happened to see if we can recreate it.'"

"That thing got us here, it can get us back!" Dr. Carstairs looked like she was about to hyperventilate.

"With respect, Doctor," Darkfeather replied, "We don't know anything about that piece of technology. For all we know, it might be a one way portal. There might be other portals on this planet that are used for outgoing travel, which means we might not have the luxury of avoiding the inhabitants here."

"I, for one," Commander Torvald interrupted, "am damn glad we came through with the assets we did. The miner, the Mark IIs, but most importantly, thank God Dora is here with us."

"Thank you, Commander. It's always nice to be appreciated."

"CAN YOU GET US HOME?" Carstairs cried out.

"Unknown at this time, Doctor."

Carstairs was obviously about to have a meltdown. Torvald interrupted her. "Dora, I believe you were in the middle of a report before we all were stunned into not listening?"

"Indeed. I mentioned the cities are of an unknown species, but they are facilities of a size that should be home to millions. However, I can only find scattered life signs within. There are more indications of similar life signs spread out over large rural areas. Though there are cities on one of the other continents, there are none of these corresponding life signs."

"Are they humanoid?"

"From what I can extrapolate from their architecture, I would say yes. However, I was almost out of the planet's gravity well to perform my scans. The exceptional solar activity currently in this star system has ionized the upper atmosphere to an extent that precise readings are very difficult."

"Well, maybe that will help with first contact," Carstairs said. "Most of the species in the Hegemony, with the exception of *Seeker's* arachnid computer expert, are humanoid–ish."

Considering one of my roommates was an insectoid, I started to comment, but Mom wasn't through with her report.

"That's not all. I also detected life signs of a humanoid species living in the oceans, and they are definitely different than the ones I found on the land, though they may possibly share some ancestry."

"Two species? Both humanoid?" Dr. Cartstairs was now distracted from her earlier panic. "There wasn't even a hint there had been sentient life on this world in the *Seeker's* scanning and in our planetary surveys. Are you sure we're on the same world?"

"I am, Doctor," Dora replied. "Consider that our original surveys also indicated that there will be a huge volcanic upheaval period around three hundred thousand years from now. If the life here now were subjected to such environmental pressures, it is not surprising that there would be vast differences in planetary life forms between geological ages. It would also indicate why we found no indication of these modern cities."

In other words, we were in an era where all sentient life would eventually go extinct. Not soon, but eventually. Everything goes extinct eventually, even my father's people, the extremely long-lived Laldoralin. But it's sobering to know of such an eventuality for certain.

"Speaking of extinct, I also found evidence of a gargantuan sea creature," Dora told us. "Immense by our standards. In our future time, there was no indication of such a creature. There is also almost no sea life that is larger than a dolphin existing in the areas it frequents."

"Suggesting it's not a cetacean plankton eater," Commander Torvald said.

"No, closer to being the much, much larger cousin of Megalodon, the gigantic shark of prehistoric Earth. I would estimate though, that it will soon be extinct. My theorem is that it has gradually eaten all of the larger sea life in the ocean, possibly including its own kind.

A being that large and carnivorous cannot exist long without prey."

"That is extremely interesting," Darkfeather said. "I wonder if…" ,

"It is interesting," Commander Torvald interrupted, "and if we were doing a scientific survey, I'd be the first one wanting to study the creature, but we have much more important fish to fry, if you'll pardon the expression. Starting with where are we going to set up for the night. As pretty as the light-show in the upper atmosphere is, I'm feeling pretty exposed out here on this plain."

"You're not the only one," Chief Moreland, still not in his suit, said. "I'm the only one here without a functioning suit, which hopefully, Dora can help me run diagnostic tests on in the morning. There's a small patch of forest to our North East. I'd suggest we find a place to work out of sight."

Chapter Eight

It was over three hours later when I finally was able to breath unrecycled air. Our Mark II suits are built for long-term survival, and aside from being able to recycle water from urine, they come with a built-in two-week allotment of nutrition paste. They also have a anti-microbial lining so that you don't choke on your own stench. But, the recycled air... It will keep you alive for weeks, but after a while you might wish you were dead.

The air in my suit hadn't gotten to that benchmark by any means, but fresh air is much preferred over suit air. We'd decided, since we were on Susanowo, it was okay to exit our armor.

I sat working with Chief Moreland, acting as executive gopher while he tried to diagnose the problem with his own Mark II. My suit stood behind me like a silent ogre, back open, ready to be re-entered at a moment's notice.

"Well, Chief," I said. "It sure looks like there's nothing wrong with the hardware."

"Yeah. I've run a diagnostic on every major piece of hardware on this baby and they all check out. That leaves a software problem. I'm gonna need Ensign Darkfeather or the Commander to see if they can source out the bad code and repair it. Until that happens, we have a very heavy paperweight here."

"With my suit and Ping's," I said, "we do have two heavy suits running. Unless someone comes after us with modern heavy weapons, we should be able to defend this position."

"And y'know, cadet," the Chief looked out toward the ocean to the west, "That is something that surprises me."

"That we have defenses?"

"No. If this gate had activated on earth, the energy surge alone would have brought someone investigating. We've been here for hours, and all we've seen is the local wildlife."

"And why are the cities so depopulated?"

"Yeah. Something is very wrong here. My guess would be some sort of plague. Dora says there are no scannable viruses that would affect us, but we've not had a chance to examine the natives. Maybe something engineered went through their population?"

"You mean," I said, "some sort of bio-weapon?" The thought was chilling. There had been no such weapon deployed on Earth since the 21st century. The rest of the Hegemony had little known usage of such weapons either, except the planet Kriox, where the Laldoralins had needed to step in aggressively to prevent planet-wide extinction.

"I certainly don't have the background to be sure, Cadet, but something is very out of whack in this place. I'm glad we have the two working suits and that your mom is flying overwatch."

"The miner bot is a pretty good resource also, even has two weeks worth of rations. And its armor makes our Mark IIs look like they're covered with paper mâché."

"Yeah, and it's a good place to put anyone who's not in a Mark II if things get hot," the chief said, setting the diagnostic scanner down. "Well, enough speculating, lets get one of our science team to see if they can find the problem in the software."

Ten minutes later, Emily Darkfeather sat down with us and had her own diagnostic device jacked into the chief's suit.

"Oh yeah," she said. "The problem is definitely software, and it's pretty glaring. Look here." She highlighted a section of the Mark II's working code displayed on her padd. "This section here, which in part governs start-up, is totally messed."

Looking over her shoulder, I could see the problem. I'm no computer expert, but everyone who goes through the academy has to have basic to mid-level programming. A large section of the suit's operating code, highlighted on her screen, looked very different from its surrounding code. There were large gaps, and several of the strings were complete gibberish.

"Well, damn." Chief Moreland said, running his fingers over his close-cropped head. "That's gonna mean a hell of a lot of hand-coding. I'll need to have a padd hooked into Junior Space Cadet's suit while I have yours on this one so I can see what the code's supposed to be."

"You're not trying to make me feel sorry enough for you to say I'll do it, are you chief?" Darkfeather asked, a grin tugging at the corners of her mouth.

"Me? I mean, just because you science kids know coding front to back and probably can do it without reference because you're so brilliant. I don't know how you thought I was trying to get you to do it."

Emily Darkfeather and I looked at each other, doing simultaneous eye rolls.

"All right, Chief," she said. "What good are officers if they can't help out their master chiefs? But with the gear we have, it's going to take a while to rebuild that entire section from scratch."

"Ensign Darkfeather," Dora's voice said via speaker, "would it not be easier to simply duplicate the section of code in Tanner's suit and replace the section that is corrupted?"

"That's a whole lot more complicated than it sounds, Dora. And all we've got to work with is a couple small science padds. I'd love to be able to just hot swap code, but it's not gonna work with these limited little computers."

"Ensign, are you forgetting that you have not only one of your Remora probes along, one of the most advanced pieces of human computational engineering, which also contains me, one of the most advanced pieces of sentient programming created by the Laldoralins? Just wondering."

I could see an embarrassed half grin on Emily's face. "I guess I'm just not used to operating with an embarrassment of riches, Dora. Do you need to come down here and jack in? The military encryption code on our hardware might prevent you from gaining access."

I heard the snort on the other end. Why an AI would ever feel the need to snort is in question, but you have to remember that an android version of Dora was acting as my mother well before humans learned they weren't alone in the cosmos. She's had plenty of practice reacting when a young person said something dumb.

"Think about it, Ensign. Where am I living these days?"

Darkfeather made the connection instantly and covered her face with her hands. "Evidently that journey through the gate scrambled my brain. Sorry, Dora."

"No worries, my dear. I can use the advanced sensors of this probe as my interface. Please don't be offended, but your Terran security measures are a thousand solar years out of date. Ah. There," Dora continued. "I have accessed Tanner's suit, copied the relevant code and am now changing individual parameters to meet the needs of Chief Moreland's suit. Accessing. Erasing old code fragment. Applying new. Chief? Please try to initiate startup."

"Holy crap. That would have taken me hours, even if I was on the *Seeker*," the Chief replied. "Hold on, let's give this a nudge and… it's rebooting. Voss, make sure the power feed from your suit is stable."

"All green, Chief."

"Here we go. Taking a charge, and… the mini-reactor is starting up! Dora, you are both awesome and scary."

"Thanks… I think?"

"And, just checking, but… are you spoken for?"

"I am flattered, Chief Moreland, but yes. I have a husband named Evan. He is fulfilling the same duties as I, watching over our daughter on the *Wanderer*."

"Ever a bridesmaid, I guess," the Chief grinned at me, reassuring me he was joking.

We had moved the chief's suit to a semi-standing position using the other Mark IIs, and now it assumed the 'stand and wait' position that was the norm for an unoccupied suit. The helmet's faceplate began to softly glow.

"It appears we have three working suits now," he said.

"That is very good timing, then," Dora said. "I am picking up several life-forms approaching your position. They will be in human visual range within one half hour."

Chapter Nine

"Chief," Dora commed us, "The first party, which appears to be the land-dwelling species, is within four hundred yards of your position. Now, however, a second contact is following them. The two groups are of different species, the second being the species most numerous in the oceans."

"Anything else you can tell us?"

"The ocean dwellers are wearing some sort of environmental armor and if I'm not mistaken, they are in pursuit of the closer group."

"So the ocean-dwellers are pursuing the land-dwellers out of the water?" Torvald asked over our comms.

"Correct. They appear to be. Aggression is sometimes difficult to interpret, but that is what appears to be happening."

"Unusual and unexpected."

"Everything about this planet and timeline is," Moreland said.

"Tanner," Commander Torvald said as he approached us. "I need for you to take scout position and get a good look at our visitors before they get here."

"Really, Commander? You want to send a cadet out there?" Chief Moreland said, exasperation dripping from his tone. "We have no idea who we're dealing with, and he's fresh out of the academy. Hell, he's not even officially out of the academy!"

"Yes, Chief. The Cadet," Commander Torvald told him. "I have seen Tanner's records from the academy. It's not general knowledge, but this young man here had the second highest combat sim scores the Terran Exploratory Force Academy has ever recorded. The only one higher was his sister, Valiel, who is on the *Wanderer*. And I and Lt. Darkfeather saw his danger sense in action on the bridge of the *Seeker*. So, yeah. The cadet."

"But Commander, the kid is so young. Hell, he'd still be at the academy if the admiral hadn't pulled strings."

Wow. I thought I'd more than proved myself, Chief.

"This is a recon mission, Chief," Torvald replied. "Just keep a low profile and everything will be fine."

"I can do this, Chief," I chimed in. "Just let me prove it. Plus, Dora will be on overwatch to catch anything I miss."

"Let me back him up, then," Moreland replied.

"Okay, chief," Commander Torvald said. "Let Voss, with his special ability, take point. You follow behind in case things get ugly."

Wearing our heavy suits, Chief Moreland and I set out in the direction that Dora indicated. The parklike flora was not great for concealment, being almost manicured in appearance.

"Voss," the chief's voice came over my comm, "your exterior faceplate is still lit. Shut it off. Make sure to switch to starlight vision."

"Yes, Chief. Starlight enabled."

"Good. Now lets go see who's coming to visit."

Our suits have both starlight vision and infrared vision but in a planetary situation like we were in starlight is by far the most useful. *Susanowo's* nighttime sky was a hundred times brighter than Earth's with two moons and a nebula. With the enhancements in my visor, it practically looked like daylight.

Dora put small different colored indicators over our HUDs where the two groups were approaching. The ocean dwellers were coming up on the land dwellers very quickly.

"Oh boy," I said. "I hope we haven't walked into someone else's war."

"Let's keep our fingers crossed, Cadet." Chief Moreland said. "I suggest we move into that copse of trees and see if we can observe without engaging."

We moved back in the foliage and knelt, no mean feat in a Mark II. We were alongside a large open field full of thigh-length grass. The light from the moon we would name 'Heaven'—500,000 years in the future—gave everything a blue-ish tint.

Had we been in the Mark III 'Godzilla' suits used by our security teams on the Seeker, we could have used the armor's adaptive camouflage, but in engineering suits we had to use the landscape to hide.

"Voss," the chief said, "I'm switching to infra-red. You stay in star-light mode. Let see if... ah. There they are, just coming into the meadow at your two o'clock. See 'em?"

"I... yes. I see them." I zoomed in with my display to get a good look. "Chief? They look a lot like Commander Pano back on the Seeker!"

"Medigin? Could be a genetic look-a-like. Mediga is way out on the other side of the Hegemony. Its civilization may be ancient, but it's incredibly far away."

The sentients that were being pursued had what looked like a vestigial dorsal fin just above their shoulder blades. Their eyes were very large and though I couldn't make out coloring using my HUD, I could at least see the webbing between their fingers. Remarkably similar our officer back on the Seeker.

"Look at their clothes," I said. "I'll bet twenty credits those are condensation suits to keep their skin moist."

As we watched, the small party of land-dwellers moved across the field, the tallest member seeming to lead the other three adults and a pair of children. Intellectually, I knew the chief was probably right. But the beings in front of us matched what I had seen of our own fellow-member race closely, even having the subtle forward body curve of the amphibious Medigin.

The universe is designed to surprise us.

"Gentlemen," Dora said over my suit's speaker, "the ocean group has evidently gotten a fix on the first party and are picking up speed. They are riding some sort of motorized foot-scooters and will be in your line of sight in a few moments."

"Foot-scooters?" Chief Moreland asked. "Commander, are you getting our visual feeds?"

"Affirmative, Chief," Torvald replied. "Dora? Why are they on conveyances? Better speed?"

"I have been able to drop to a lower altitude for better scanning of both parties, Commander," Dora told him. "The secondary group are not amphibians as the first groups is. These beings are all wearing some sort of environmental suit. They are true aquatics and as such have feet more akin to scuba flippers. The mechanized vehicles they are riding allow them to cover land at a much increased rate over what they would be able to accomplish unassisted."

That made sense. When I was a kid, I once tried to hurry from our picnic area to the local lake. Saving time, I'd donned my flippers first and headed out at a lope. It took a while to pick the grass out of my teeth.

"I see the aquatics now," I said. "They're moving fast on the amphibs."

As we watched, the pursuers, whose glistening black armor prevented us from getting a good look at them, stopped and raised what looked like lances. As one, they fired and a shimmering projectile streaked toward their prey. It hit one of the larger amphibs in the back and in an amazing spray of water knocked him off his feet and a good twenty feet ahead. He landed on his face and lay still.

"Damn!" Chief Moreland said. "Whatever they shot at them it sure packs a punch. Looked like some sort of compressed liquid contained in an energy field projectile."

The remaining amphibians turned and raised their arms in, what looked like to me, a pleading gesture, as if begging the sea-dwellers to not fire again. The second aquatic immediately fired its weapon and two of the adult amphibians went flying. I started to rise, hating to see such an attack go unanswered.

"Cadet," Moreland growled, "stay put. We have no idea what the situation is here."

"Yes, Chief. But it seems pretty obvious that those black-armored bastards are hunting the group with the kids in their midst. That's not right."

"We're not even supposed to be here. Let's not get in a fight with no idea who's who, capiche?"

"Understood."

The remaining two adults were cowering, covering their heads, trying to move in front of the children when they were knocked flying by two more shots from the creatures on the scoots. This left just the kids, and I dreaded seeing them hit with the weapon that had just floored all the adults in their group. I doubted the small ones would be able to survive such a hit.

It was all I could do to obey orders and sit still.

Both of the black armored creatures rolled up to the down and out amphibians and got off their scoots. They unrolled what looked like golden nets, and began to drag the adults onto them. When they had them all, one of the sea-dwellers hit some sort of control and the net contracted around their unconscious prey.

"I guess they're going to put the kids on the scooters with them," Moreland whispered through my comm.

"We don't know that!"

One of the two sea creatures walked over to the kids, looking over each one as if trying to decide something. It then touched a spot on its armor, and the helmet it wore folded away into the body, revealing a horror-show face. I mean that literally.

When I was a kid, I loved old monster movies from the 20th century and the monstrosity that was revealed was a dead ringer for the old Creature from the Black Lagoon. There were a few differences, the fin that unfurled on the top of his head like a mohawk or the rows of needle teeth in the fishlike mouth, but its head at least was familiar-looking.

But as it reached down and grabbed one of the kids by an arm it did something the old rubber suit movie-monster had never done. It grinned. Evilly. That may seem like a subjective analysis, but the creature's next move proved me right.

The sea creature calmly reached down with its face and bit a chunk out of the child's arm.

The high-pitched squeal of the kid's scream was like a dolphin in distress and I turned toward Moreland to tell him he could sit on his neutrality. But as I turned, I realized I was alone in the little copse of trees. Looking back toward the field I saw a juggernaut moving like a lineman in an old-world football game, tufts of sod flying up behind. The chief must've hit his boiling point, because his neutrality was out the window.

He ran up on the being who'd bitten the child, and swinging one heavy metal gauntlet, he hit the creature dead center in its chest. My external microphone picked up the sound of the crushing impact as the enemy went flying off into the grass.

Go Chief!

I was up and moving as the second creature grabbed its weapon and swung it around to aim at Moreland. Guttural sounds rose from its glass-fronted helmet, sounds both liquid and coarse at the same time.

I was still too far away to do anything, and the chief had only just turned toward his second adversary. It fired at his chest at almost point blank range. The weapon indeed had some punch, as it rocked the Mark II suit back on its heels, but Chief Moreland recovered quickly and advanced on his attacker with great menace in his approach.

The sea-dweller jumped on his scoot and headed back toward the ocean at top speed.

"Dora," Moreland said, "did you catch all that?"

"Affirmative, Chief. Your surviving enemy is speeding away and is almost a quarter mile distant at this point."

"I need overwatch. I'm going to egress from my suit and see if I can render first aid on this little kid. Hopefully I won't terrify him into an aneurysm. Cadet, watch my back."

"Aye aye, Chief."

The back of Moreland's Mark II opened up and he climbed out the back. He opened up a small locker on the suit's left thigh and pulled out the exterior emergency kit (well marked as such) and snapped it open.

"Here's hoping these beings are as close to our Mediga allies as they look," he said. The chief slapped a med-ball on the bleeding, gaping wound and it shaped itself to fit. Blood vessels were closed off, re-routed through bio-gel and antibiotics administered.

The child, oddly enough, looked at Moreland with what I can only ascribe as wonder. Its huge gel-tear-filled eyes didn't show any of the panic I'd seen earlier. It vocalized sing-song sounding words that must've been a attempt to communicate with us.

"Dora, can you scan the kid from up there? Is the bio-gel working, or is his tissue rejecting it?" The chief asked.

"Let me tighten resolution, I am currently at ten-thousand feet from the surface. Ah, it appears that the bio-gel is working as intended. My scans, being quite thorough, have penetrated to the cellular level and what I have found is most astonishing."

"Elaborate, please."

"One moment, I am ensuring Commander Torvald and Ensign Darkfeather are linked in. Commander? Do you copy?"

"I'm here, Dora. Darkfeather too. Tell the chief that he and I will be having a discussion of what neutrality means."

"Yes, sir. I'd like to add Dr. Carstairs also. Her disciplines will also be of use in this situation." Dora added.

"Hell, add everyone. We're a team, and withholding information is only going to be counterproductive."

"What have you found, Dora?" Dr. Carstairs said.

"The chief and cadet Voss have been in an altercation between the amphibian race and the aquatic race. I have scanned some unconscious amphibians to a deep cellular-level degree, and can only come to one conclusion. These people are not just similar to our Medigan allies, they are of an almost identical gene pool."

Chapter Ten

"How I wish Lt. Commander Pano was here," Dr. Carstairs said, brushing a strand of her flaming red hair aside. "We have one Medigan crew member on the entire ship, and it would be very helpful if these beings could see a familiar looking face when they regain consciousness."

'Well ma'am," Chief Moreland replied. "I'm not sure how to make a comm call 500,000 years into the future, but if I can figure it out he'll be the first person I call,"

"Very droll, Chief. My doctorate is in xeno-archaeology but I've had occasion on remote sites to realize that I needed med-tech training. From the best I can tell from the scans Dora's sending me, their injuries will be painful but not life-threatening. It seems the aquatic species wanted the amphibian species alive."

"That in itself provides a number of images that I don't want in my head," Ensign Darkfeather said. "The way that thing took a bite out of that kid. Did it with delight as far as I could tell." I shuddered as she said it.

"It was pure evil, as far as I'm concerned," I said.

"Well, "Commander Torvald said, "In any event, we're in it now. Dora? When these people come around, they'll probably be talking to each other…"

"I will build a linguistic base for our translators, Commander. If they are talkative, it should not take long for me to establish a baseline and build from there. Once that's established, our comms should be able to function as translators."

"Once again, damn thankful you're with us."

The adult amphibs had started to come around, though they were obviously a bit worse for wear. Dora's scans of the weapon we'd commandeered from the aquatics showed that they were not only impact-based but had a taser-like effect in the containment field of each charge.

As the adults seemed finally aware and awake, I was surprised to see the young ones emphatically gesturing at us. It seemed like excitement, but I knew caution was needed when trying to apply human interactions to unknown alien species.

The adults were talking amongst themselves, in a rolling musical language and I was a little surprised they weren't freaking out at the sight of us alien beings. They weren't speaking modern Medigin, though. If they had been our translation matrix would've been giving us realtime translated speech from the get-go.

I imagined what the reaction would've been a couple hundred years prior if these people had shown up out of the blue on Earth. For now, they were only keeping a wary eye on us and listening to what their kids were telling them about us.

"They seem to be handling things well, considering we must be extremely foreign to anything they've seen before," I said as I did a little adjusting to my suit's gyro system.

"It could be weariness, or adrenaline fatigue," Commander Torvald replied. "Dora? Do you have an estimate on how many beings the cities that you've scanned might reasonably house?"

"Not by any means an exact number, but each could've easily been home to a million or more adult sentients." Dora told him. "However, there are only a few lifeforms in the cities I have scanned. Each metropolis seems to be without power and are for the most part deserted."

"Which says to me," Dr. Carstairs said, "that this has been going on for a while now. Think about it. Millions of people going missing would take a while. If these sea-dwellers are behind it, and they are capturing these people I can't imagine the logistics needed. I'm sure it isn't something that could be done in a short time." She looked toward the amphibians. "Which also says these people have been on the run for a long time."

"I can't imagine what that must be like, running for one's life, just one step ahead of being massacred," Ensign Darkfeather said, shaking her head. "Why would the sea-dwellers do this? It has all the trappings of a genocide."

"The way that one took a bite I wonder if they're being rounded up like cattle," I said.

"Dora? Any progress on that translation program?" Torvald asked.

"I assure you commander, as soon as I have something workable I will let you know," I detected a hint of mildly irritated mom-voice in her reply. "There are also certain subjects that are going to take longer than normal conversation. Spacecraft or time travel as subjects are going to take quite a bit longer than discussions about the weather."

"Sorry. I didn't mean to step on your non-existent toes, there."

"I expect to be able to have a basic conversation matrix with our guests here within the hour."

This entire time, Dora was sitting at around 5,000 feet above us keeping an eye on our surrounding. The Remora probes were intended to be able to provide high-resolution sensor data from planetary system distances. Multi-tasking this way was child's play to her.

"Doctor Carstairs?" Darkfeather asked. "What is your take on the length of time this has been going on? The depopulation of the cities, I mean."

"If these sea-dwellers have been rounding up everyone they can get, it's hard to say. The first place the oppressors would go would be large population centers. If these people, amphibs, as you call them, had no viable defense... If I were in their shoes I'd desert the cities rather quickly."

"That suggests the sea-dwellers may exist in numbers that are overwhelming," Chief Moreland said. "We've not exactly been dropped into an optimal situation here. Who knows, maybe those sea-bastards might want to try some exotic alien cuisine."

"Damn, Chief," Ensign Teo, still in her Mark II, exclaimed though her external speakers. "Now I won't sleep for, oh... I dunno... forever!"

"If any of this winds up fitting the facts of the situation, and we are still conjecturing, then whatever happened we've probably chosen a side in this war," Ensign Darkfeather said. "I can't see us siding with a bunch of sentient-eating piranha faces like those in your video record. Might as well be allying with velociraptors."

We all sat, digesting that particular thought, as the amphibians murmured amongst themselves.

"Please monitor your speech from this point on," Dora said. "I am about to feed what you are saying into my translation matrix so that we can begin communicating with these people. Translations will be rough, but will rapidly improve, the more that you converse."

◆

How do you approach people with whom you have no common frame of reference? I guess the stock answer is slowly and gently, if you are not already hostile to each other. The amphibs looked up as we approached, the one who'd been keeping a close eye on us alerting all the others.

They weren't unpleasant to look at. Hairless, with sleek gray-blue skin, and in the illumination of Minnie the Miner's various lamps and spotlights, their large oval eyes were a spectrum of gem-like blue and purple. They had elfin looking faces, with narrow chins and wide cheekbones. They reminded me a little of anime characters in Japanese cartoons. As the commander approached them, they all rose to their feet.

"We," Torvald began, "are not from your world."

Fast chuffs came from their mouths, and their shoulders shook while they made the sounds. The sounds weren't loud, weren't given with much enthusiasm, but unless all the signs were wrong, some of them were... laughing?

"If I'm not mistaken, sir," Darkfeather said. "I believe that was the equivalent of 'no shit, Sherlock.'"

"Please monitor your verbalizations, Ensign," Dora reminded her.

"Oops, sorry, Dora."

Commander Torvald continued as if nothing else had been said. "We wish to be friends." The amphibs looked down at the padd on his belt, where the translation was being broadcast.

"Our littles," a smaller male said, standing up and coming closer, "say you friends. Say you hit Ravrath. Who are you?"

"We are from there," Torvald said, pointing up to the stars.

It's difficult to interpret the expressions of an alien species, because the only reference point we have is human expressions. (And the other aliens we have encountered.) Even then we don't always correctly interpret the expressions of our own species. The amphib seemed to grow agitated and looked to his companions. A series of complex noises came from his mouth and the translator couldn't keep up.

Finally he looked back at Torvald and said slowly and clearly, "Take us away from here. Where is your craft?" He looked skeptical as he gave Minnie the Miner a closer look. "This is it?"

"No," Torvald replied, "This is not a star craft. Our ship..." he seemed at a loss for words. How to explain that our starship was 500,000 years in the future? "We came through that." He pointed up the hill toward the huge arch that stood in silhouette against the borealis effect.

Half of the amphibian group jumped to their feet. If the translator had had problems keeping up before, it became useless in the face of their excited chatter. They spoke amongst themselves for a while, then the original speaker returned to Torvald and slowly and carefully spoke his next words.

"Our colony is a success?"

"Your colony?"

"Yes. We sent through three waves. Almost... er... many, many of our people," he told us. "The last wave was unsure. Much..." he pointed toward the glow where the star sat below the horizon, then waved at the continuous "Northern Lights" display going on above our heads.

Dora supplied the words, "interference from the star's emissions, Commander."

"We received... call... transmissions from first two waves," the amphibians told us, "but none from the third. Did you find them?"

I had a remembrance of thousands of skeletons sitting under Minnie's treads when we were about to be sucked through the gate. Somehow, it looked like wave three hadn't gone where it was supposed to.

"We did find them, we believe," Torvald told him. "But the news is not good. When we were pulled through, we were there." He pointed at the sulphurous moon passing overhead.

Our guest's mouth dropped open and a high pitched soft whine emerged from it. "Ohhhh, this is terrible news. No one could have lived up there."

"I am deeply sorry," Torvald told him. "There is one other thing you should know, but I must ask if you are a scientist who understands the device." He again pointed toward the portal sitting alone out on the plain.

His question seemed to be lost on the amphib. Not because of Dora's translation matrix, which seemed to be getting better moment by moment, but he was staring at the gate with what could only be described as 'the thousand mile stare' in a human.

"I forgot to introduce myself," the commander said, trying to bring the sentient back into the here and now. "I am Torvald. I lead this group." He gestured to the rest of us.

Our guest looked up. "I… I am Givall. And yes, I am a scientist and was one of the leads on…" he gestured to where the arch stood, "..that. My associates and I were trying to see if there there was any way to restore power to it. We picked up a few others along the way. What was the thing you said I should know?"

"We," Torvald told him, a slight hesitancy in his tone, "are from the far future of this world. We entered the arch many, many, many orbits from now."

I could see Givall trying to form a question, but the enormity of the commander's statement had left him seemingly speechless. "Please restate. I might have misunderstood."

"We," Torvald gestured toward our people, "live over five hundred thousand orbits from now. The portal pulled us back into your time period."

"How is that possible?" one of the female amphibs asked. "The Shelar is a spacial trans-locator, it has nothing to do with traveling through time!" Dora's translation matrix sounded like it had made a leap of light years.

"Could the interference… no, that can't be," Givall said. "That's not possible!"

"Well, if it's not possible, we wouldn't be here," Torvald told him. "You can put it down to cosmic chance, science gone wrong or divine intervention if you wish. Nonetheless, we've been dropped here in the middle of your war."

Chapter Eleven

Eventually, Givall introduced his associates and family members. A few of the group were stragglers that his team had picked up along the way. The woman who had spoken earlier was his mate, a fellow scientist named Lallal. She was tall, and had an elegantly long neck that curved slightly forward away from the vestigial dorsal fin just below it.

He had two children, the one's we'd saved. The girl named Kipo, the boy named Zatta. Kipo was a shy kid, and stayed behind her mother's legs. Zatta, slightly larger than his sister, was the one who'd been chomped on and he kept rubbing the bio-gel where he'd been bitten.

The other two adults were a male named Datt and a young female named Sikal. Both had been trying to find safety from the sea-dwelling Ravrath when they were found by Givall and company. Sikall was slender and her dorsal fin was small compared to Lallal's I didn't know if that was a function of age or just genetics. Datt on the other hand, was bulky and the vestigial dorsals on his back and forearms were quite pronounced. He didn't seem inclined to join the conversation.

The scientist had promised to help them reach a citadel where most of their species (named Dohannen) were making a last stand.

We of the *Seeker* contingent introduced ourselves as well, and there were minor difficulties with them assuming our rank was part of our names. The Dohannen's military forces, what was left of them, used a different rank system that evidently bore little resemblance to ours.

Eventually, they understood that Cadet was not my name.

"It is hard to believe that you are here, just at our darkest moment," Sikal said as she sat with us. Torvald, Darkfeather, Givall and Lalal had gone a ways off from the miner to discuss the gate, and if there was any way it could be used to get us all out of our current predicaments. "I am not what you would call a religious being, but one could almost imagine your presence was commanded by the Six Gods."

"I would love to hear more about your mythology," Dr. Carstairs told her. "Do these six deities work in tandem or in opposition?"

"Supposedly, they work together," Sikal said. "Watching over all of our people and directing the workings of all our people. Were that true, we must've really fouled the nets, considering what has happened to us over the last five orbits."

"What exactly is going on here?" Chief Moreland asked. "We seem to have emerged into the middle of a war between you and these Ravrath creatures."

"A war?" Datt, sitting off to the side on some crates, gave a bitter laugh. "This is not a war, this is a *shika zarra*," the translation caught up, "..a genocide. They are wiping us Dohannen out."

"Why would they do that?" I asked. "Do they want your lands? Your crops? Technology?"

"None of those, Cadet..er.. sorry, I mean Tanner," Sikal said. "You could at least see a reason for those however evil that reason might be. They round up those of us they can still catch, drag us down to the shores of the great mother ocean and feed us to the leviathan."

Dora's voice came from my padd speaker, "That must be the gigantic lifeform that I detected earlier from orbit. Is there only one?"

"As far as anyone knows," Datt said. "To whom am I speaking?"

"I am Dora, an artificial intelligence supporting the team of earth people that you are conversing with. I am housed in a sensor probe hovering approximately 5,000 feet above you." The translator made a strange word-sound for the measurement which I could only assume was translating feet into whatever measurement was closest.

How would she get that information though?

"Dora?" I asked. "Are you tapping into Dohannen information nets?"

"Yes, Tanner. There are some deep-buried installations, military of some sort, that have large computer systems still running. They have vast data-bases, but I am only delving into anything we might find useful, at this point."

"Just like that? There's no security?"

Dora's tone became a little condescending, "Really Tanner, these are primitive systems compared to my own. Bypassing security is child's play."

"Forgive us," Dr. Carstairs said. "Dora is an autonomous being, and sometimes forgets that maybe permission should be asked before accessing other people's information."

"If I have erred," Dora said. "Please accept my apologies. I believed that accessing your data-bases might prove beneficial in helping our two groups integrate so that we might work together to solve our problems."

Was that just the teeniest bit of snark in that answer? She's my mom, and I have to say... probably.

"It is no longer important, Sikal said. "As a species, we will probably be wiped from existence soon. Take all you want, Dora. It might be the only record of us to survive."

◆

"Sir?" I said, as Commander Torvald walked over to us, "Dora has breached the main data-base for the Dohannen. She has some interesting insights."

"Talk to me Dora."

"Commander, from what I have learned, this action by the Ravrath against the Dohannen is less than five years old. The surviving population of our amphibious friends is currently at around twenty thousand individuals, though I have not verified this with detailed scanning."

"I sense a big 'and' coming here, Dora."

"Census before the war had the Dohannen population at almost 1.2 billion individuals."

It took a moment for the commander to process this huge discrepancy, but when he did, he looked up into the sky as if he could see Dora's Remora probe 5,000 feet above us.

'Dora, are you saying…"

"Yes Commander, the Ravrath have decimated the Dohannen and are on a track to bring them to extinction. Even with twenty thousand people remaining, I would calculate that their genetic diversity has been severely compromised."

"What did they do with all the dead?" Torvald said, distress showing in his expression. "My God, a billion beings…"

"They fed them," Givall said as he joined us. "to the Karemora. The Leviathan. You notice you're not seeing bodies lying around or smelling the stink of death. All protein for the great beast."

"They just decided to sacrifice you all? Just like that?"

"We have been at conflict with the Ravrath for much of our history. We were prey for them. At one point, long ago our species literally left the oceans behind to become land dwellers simply to put an end to our constant wars."

"Did that work?" I asked.

"We have been at peace, though an uneasy peace, for over four hundred orbits," Givall replied. "Though we've never trusted each other, we've developed trading partnerships with them and negotiated access to certain parts of the seas. The Ravrath have shown little interest in coming on land, though perhaps that was a subterfuge. Many of our people were taken with vehicles that they must've been developing for generations to attack land-based population centers."

"How long has this Leviathan been a problem?" Dr. Carstairs asked. "Is it some sort of deity to the Ravrath?"

"The Leviathan, the Karemora, first showed up on our scans eleven orbits ago," Givall replied. "I do not know if it has religious significance." He shuddered, "All I know is that survivors who escaped have said the Ravrath line their captives on the shore, then force them into the ocean with their water weapons. The Leviathan creates a big wave, that when it reverses, drags all the victims into it's huge maw."

"If I may interject, Commander?" Dora asked.

"Interject away, Dora."

"My scans indicate that there is a new volcano approximately seven hundred miles out in the ocean and it appears to have been caused by recent seismic activity. I am theorizing, but it is possible this awoke a titan that had been hibernating on or in the ocean floor."

We looked at Givall, and he made a gesture with his head, moving it to one side. When we continued to look without speaking, he realized we didn't understand what he meant. "We've all had theories on where it came from, and that one seems as good as any."

"To continue theorizing," Dora said. "My scans of the immediate areas of the nearby ocean indicate no life form larger than a terrestrial dolphin. No large cetaceans, or large cephalopods, nor any of the large shark-like creatures that have been found on every aquatic world. The only creatures of any size are those who hug the reef systems or who live very close to shore."

"I think I see where you're going with this, Dora," Torvald said. "You think this thing is cleaning out the oceans. And since the oceans are all linked, and not blocked by overly large continents there's literally nowhere for large lifeforms to run."

"Yes, commander. That leads me to believe that this genocide of the Karemora is not a holy Jihad, but a short-sighted attempt at self-preservation on the part of the Ravrath."

"They're sacrificing the Dohannen to keep the Leviathan from eating them?" I said. "Aside from the fact that they're rapidly running out of Dohannen, wouldn't they need to somehow bargain with the creature to make that work."

Givall made a noise. He looked off towards the ocean thoughtfully. "The ones who survived, that brought their stories back to us, said they felt a hunger coming from the ocean. They felt something was telling them not to resist. They said it was very compelling and that only a few were able to overcome it."

"Telepathic?" Dr. Carstairs said. "Intelligent?"

"It is a distinct possibility, Doctor," Dora replied.

Chapter Twelve

We spent the rest of that night learning about each other, but eventually, we split into two camps. I slept at the foot of my Mark II, while Ping and the Chief kept watch in their suits. Dora had overwatch and thankfully didn't have to sleep. Dr. Carstairs, Ensign Darkfeather and Commander Torvald slept in Minnie's narrow bunks, though they'd given all the miner's blankets to the Dohannen.

It was almost dawn, the borealis in the sky was starting to fade, when Ping tapped me on the shoulder to say it was my watch. "Come on Tanner, rise and shine, Sunshine."

"Guh," I said, trying to rub the sleepiness out of my eyes. "Is there coffee?"

"Does this look like the New Pheonix Hilton? I thought all that fancy pantsy Laldoralin DNA would make you spring out of bed with vigor and a song in your heart."

Thinking of songs I'd like to sing at Ensign Teo, many of them from the 21st century and none of them polite, I merely shrugged. "Half-Laldoralin. My human DNA makes me wake up like any regular human. Grumpily."

'Well, get up Grumpy. The chief told me I can't get out of my suit until you get into yours."

"Aye, aye, Ma'am."

"And you can ditch the 'Ma'am' stuff cadet. I AM only two years older than you, y'know, plus or minus a hundred and fifty."

That got a laugh out of me, though a brief one. I splashed some water we'd collected from a nearby stream on my face, then went over to a swath of trees and peed. Moments later, my Mark II was sealing itself around me.

"Okay Ping, I'm green. Nap time for you."

"Wish it was shower time. I'm setting my suit to sanitize mode while I'm sleeping. Things are starting to get a little whiffy in there."

"Yeah," I said. "I did the same. Unless we can get some kind of place to stay, maybe in one of those abandoned cities, it's not gonna get better."

"Well hopefully the Commander is taking that into account. I feel very exposed out here, Dora's overwatch not withstanding."

"Speaking of which," I said, "how's it going up there, Mom?"

"At this time, I am detecting no patrols of the Ravrath in your vicinity, Tanner. There is one approximately twenty miles to the southwest and I am detecting some sort of heavy vehicle with said patrol. It seems to be armed with unknown weaponry. I have also informed the Chief. From what I am hearing inside the miner, I believe the commander and Ensign Darkfeather are also awake. I will inform them also."

"Everyone," Commander Torvald's voice came over the transceiver a few minutes later, "let's meet in front of Minnie. We need to start formulating a game plan."

"Guh," Ping said. "So much for a nap."

◆

"We can't stay here." Commander Torvald gestured toward the open plain beyond our copse of trees. "Dora calculates that the Ravrath patrols have a ninety percent chance of eventually stumbling over us."

"Considering how the chief took out one of their patrols," Ensign Darkfeather said, "may be that's not as big a worry as we think."

"If I may interject, Commander," Dora's voice transmitted, "the patrol Chief Moreland encountered was a small one, obviously intended to round up stray Dohannen. I have noted larger patrols, armed with heavier equipment and I must assume heavier weapons. I endorse your strategy of finding a place to hide. You are equipped with mining and engineering equipment, and though it is robust, it is not intended for military use."

"Oh, God," Torvald said, running his hands through his thick brown hair, "how I wish Chief Kurakin was here. She has more combat experience than anyone else on the *Seeker*, by far."

"Um.. sir?" I said. "There is one among us who has a lot of combat experience because of..."

"Tanner!" Mom's voice quite sternly called. "The Commander is quite cognizant of what you are about to speak of, but you will remember that information has been limited to high-ranking officials and military commanders on Earth. For very good reasons."

"Oh.. uh... right."

"Sir," Darkfeather said, "what is she talking about?"

Torvald looked off toward the distant ocean, sighed, and seemed to come to a decision. "We are almost five hundred thousand years in the past. What I am about to tell you, should we be fortunate enough to return to our own time, is not to be discussed with anyone among the *Seeker's* crew or civilians. I am including you in this, Dr. Carstairs. If you won't swear to keep it quiet if we return, then go into the miner and I will come get you when we're done."

'Commander Torvald," Carstairs answered. "I can keep a secret when necessary. I hereby swear that I will not share whatever information you're about to impart. But... what about him?"

Givall had walked up, seeing we were deep in discussion. "Please forgive me," he said, "but I believe our fates are now intertwined. If you are able to return to your future, we'd very much like to accompany you. I will swear on my life if that happens that I will keep your information safe."

The commander stood without answering for a moment, then nodded his head. Realizing the Dohannen scientist might not understand that, he said, "Our survival and yours is most likely if we don't keep secrets, though I'm not sure that this one will affect you or your people right now. As for the future, who knows how that will go."

"People," he continued, "we've all heard about the wonders and benefits of being part of the Laldoralin Hegemony. They stopped Earth from engaging in constant battle and made us see humanity as one race. They've uplifted us, given us technology that has mostly offset the environmental mistakes of our ancestors, and gifted us with star-travel. However, as young Tanner obviously knows due to his familial connection, the galaxy is not all wine and roses."

"Thiiiisss... doesn't sound good," Ensign Teo said.

"It isn't, Ensign. What only our leaders and military commanders know is that the Laldoralins uplifted us, not to bring us out to the stars, but to eventually be able to protect ourselves."

"But I thought the Hegemony was a truly stable part of the galaxy," Chief Moreland said.

"For the most part, but... well... Dora? Can you take it from here?" Torvald asked.

"Affirmative, Commander. Part of the reason the Laldoralin are set on helping the younger races accelerate their growth is that the older races have been waging on-again/off-again wars with three different predatory races. The one closest to Earth, would be the Klugg, a world-devouring race of parasitical beings who have destroyed all the larger life-forms on more than one world."

"But.. why didn't they let the general public know?" Darkfeather asked.

"Consider the trepidation of some groups on Earth, Ensign," Dora said. "Even to this day, there are people adamantly opposed to space travel and interaction with non-Terrans. The *Seeker's* sister ship was destroyed by a member of Earth for Earth. We have one of their saboteurs in our brig. The human race has come far and fast and many are frightened of the change. Talking about great dangers that your people might have to defend themselves from might've induced large portions of humanity to dig a hole and pull it in after them."

"Yeah," Dr. Carstairs said. "I can totally see that."

"This information will be forthcoming after Earth's inhabitants have spent one hundred solar orbits as a space-faring species. However, none of this information is relevant to our current situation."

"Maybe only tangentially, Dora," Torvald said, "but I believe your son was intending a point much more... on point?"

"Commander, I only wanted to inform you that Dora has a lot of combat experience," I said. "I didn't mean to open this whole other can of worms. I was thinking that maybe she could lead us if it comes to combat."

"Totally inappropriate suggestion, Cadet," Chief Moreland said.

"I didn't mean all the time…"

"It is, nonetheless, improper, Tanner," Dora said. "It is a contravention of the chain of command. I would however like to offer my services as tactical advisor, Commander Torvald. As my son states I am very experienced. I've commanded drone ships, drone forces and robotic infantry. Remotely, of course."

"Dora, I will gladly take suggestions from you. Don't hesitate," Torvald said. "I've had a good deal of standard officer military training, but my specialty is science, not guerrilla fighting. And make no mistake, we are an insurgency. If we're not willing to fight these Ravrath, they'll make short work of us."

"You will not be completely alone," Givall said, stepping closer. "Though from the outside it may look like my people are helpless and non-resisting, we have an "insurgency," as you call it. We have covert fighting forces strung throughout the countryside. The Ravrath have also been unable to break the defenses of our last remaining military base which is located under a mountain. The vast tunnel system there are where the majority of my remaining people have retreated to."

"Is it far from here?" Torvald asked.

"Yes, it would be a full day of travel on foot, unless your miner unit is a lot faster on land than it looks."

"It's designed for use in space, mostly," Chief Moreland told him. "Not terribly fast at land travel, though faster than the average human can run."

"Which says to me," Torvald said, "we need someplace closer to go to ground. Let's pack up folks. We're goin' to the big city."

Chapter Thirteen

The city of Kaniber was beautiful, if you tried not to notice the parts that'd been damaged by weapons fire.

Unlike human cities, which tended toward boxiness and straight lines, the Dohanen city had a water-like flow. It was all curves, with great gleaming buildings that put me in mind of a dolphin's dorsal fin. The upper areas of the buildings were immaculate but at street level, things were a different story. The long slashing burns from energy weapons wrote a deadly calligraphy across buildings, shattering windows and melting metal.

The streets consisted of a hard rubbery material that unfortunately seemed to stain easily. The stains were a reddish purple color, and I didn't think for a moment that it was some sort of oil. There were gleaming surfaces every where, though they seemed a bit dusty and colorful murals made of tiny mosaic tiles.

At the base of the buildings, usually where the weapons burns drew horizontally across, lay the the bisected and scorched remains of Ravrath soldiers, their weapons lying beside them. The decay of the bodies told us they'd been killed some weeks ago. The stench was quite… unpleasant.

"Is it just me," Ensign Teo said over comms, "or are the only bodies from the fish people. I don't see any of Givall's people lying here."

"That's weird," I replied. "The Ravs were just left where they fell."

"Grab up any of their weapons you see, Cadet," Chief Moreland said, his armored suit a hundred yards ahead of us, taking point. "All our personal tools we can use as weapons are very short range. We need anything we can get to put up a fight, even if it's the weaponry of our enemies."

A pair of Ravrath bodies lay against a nearby wall. Both had dropped their weapons, though one energy staff had been bisected with its owner. I picked up the other.

"I have no idea how this thing shoots," I said.

"At the back," Lallal said. We had keyed her and Givall into our general frequency and given them extra hand-held comm units from the locker in the miner. "You will see a part of the staff that protrudes slightly, just before the end curls downward. That is a trigger mechanism."

"Chief, request permission to try this thing out."

A chuckle came over my mic. "All right, cadet. Give it a shot and be careful of your target. Make sure it's something that won't piss off our friends."

A superior in my chain of command had just given me the go-ahead to fire off an alien weapon I knew nothing about. The day was looking up.

Aiming toward a vehicle laying on its side, I pulled the trigger with my first two fingers. An oval of liquid appeared on the other end of the staff and a static charge built around it just before it moved toward the target. The charged liquid hit the car, denting it and rocking it slightly.

"Well, that might knock someone over, but I gotta say I'm not impressed."

"Hold the the trigger for a count of four and try again," Lalal said.

'Will do," I replied. I aimed the weapon again, this time holding the trigger for a count of five, just to be sure. When I released it the charged liquid hit the vehicle and instead of slightly rocking it caused the entire thing to flip over in mid air and land on its opposite side. The crash resounded through the empty canyon of buildings. "Oh. That's impressive."

"And noisy," Ping said. "Please, let's not tell the Rav where we are."

"Team," Torvald said, "Givall says that the best place to hide Minnie and also have room to work would be that building ahead and to the right. It's some sort of sports arena and it looks like the main entrance is large enough for our miner bot to get in without scraping the sides."

We moved to the structure, which like all of the buildings around it was built along flowing lines that were not symmetrical as they would've been on earth. There were not as many windows as most of the surrounding structures but its base was far larger than the others and more lake-shaped for lack of a better word. It was well over a Terran city block in diameter.

We wirelessly supplied power to the main door. It was constructed of metal slats that rotated sideways, then rose into the ceiling. The commander then drove Minnie inside into a large open area containing several large vehicles that looked as if they were some sort of haulers.

"Dora? Can you still read us out there?"

"Aye Commander. The building is offering no substantial lessening of comms but scans are sketchy. I am detecting no new life signs in your selected structure, but I recommend an in-person recon."

"That's good to know. Okay people, Moreland and Teo, you can exit your suits and take a rest. Darkfeather, you know how to run a Mark II, don't you?"

"Aye Commander. I might be a bit rusty, but I've had the training."

"Good. Patrol the lower levels and see if we're alone. Cadet, since you were the last suit jockey to get a rest, I'd like you to escort Dr. Carstairs around the building and see what we have to work with. Try to find us a good observation point in the upper levels. Also, see if there are any food establishments in the building. Our own supplies are going to dwindle quickly with this many of us. Minnie's rations were intended for a two-person team for three weeks. Hopefully, Dora can scan local cuisine for edibility. And be vigilant."

"Understood sir. Doctor? Are you ready for some sight seeing?"

"Yes," Carstairs replied, "if you think you can maneuver that huge suit of armor inside this place, let's go see what we can find."

◆

The building was immense, and dim lighting continued to illuminate the hall ways. I quickly saw that our exploration wasn't going to be quick or particularly easy. I was fortunate in that most of the main hallways were intended for crowds and posed no difficulty to my bulky suit's maneuverability.

"I wonder what sort of sporting events they had here," I said through my suit speakers.

"This was an aquatic arena," someone said from behind us. We turned and found that Sikall, the young Dohannen female had joined us. She looked at us for a moment, then said; "I thought you aliens might need a local guide to figure out what was what. Do you mind if I tag along? I'd like to help if I can, if for any other reason, to just not feel so useless."

It was amazing to me, that with a race we'd never encountered just how similar feelings could run.

"Of course you can come with us," Dr. Carstairs said, a warm tone in her voice, "unless tin-can man here has some objection."

"Happy for the help," I said. "So, aquatic sports?"

"If you go to the center of the arena," Sikall said, "you'll see a huge pool. Our people may have been forced from the oceans hundreds of orbits ago, but we still base our society around water. Races, trophy capturing, and other activities that remind us of who we once were."

"Ocean-dwellers," the doctor said.

"Ocean-dwellers. A heritage stolen from us by the Ravrath."

"What can you tell us about your history with them, Sikall?" Carstairs asked they young Dohannen.

"It was never particularly good. I'm not old enough to remember when we could freely swim the oceans, but I still feel the loss down somewhere deep within me." Sikall told us. "Our people have always had a bad relationship with the Rav, they've constantly tried to prey upon us, though nothing like what we're seeing today. When we were in the ocean, we always swam in large groups. Those who were alone were attacked and usually eaten. Our technology protected us to some degree, but the Dohannen eventually grew tired of always having to be on guard. We moved to the land and only swim in the fresh water places now."

"You've built a remarkable civilization in a very short time," Carstairs said.

"We had excellent technology before we left. That helped us move here. But we always longed for the ocean. Unfortunately, anyone who tried to return to the seas usually disappeared, taken by the Rav. I think they missed eating us."

"That's awful," I said.

"How… how I hate them." Sikall looked down at the smooth floor. "And now, as if stealing our birthright wasn't enough, they've decided we're not worthy of existence."

"They must realize that if they destroy all of you," I said, "this Leviathan thingie is going after them next. Then I guess that the following step is it goes extinct from starvation. Do your remaining people have any sort of large bomb they could drop down this monster's throat from an aircraft?"

"A what?" Sikall said. Evidently there was a hiccup in the translation matrix.

"Uh.. you know, a vehicle that flies through the air?" She looked at me with a blank expression. "Sikall, do you mean to tell me that a society as advanced as yours doesn't have air travel?"

"No! That is a thing of avians. We are not avians."

"Fascinating," Dr. Carstairs interjected. "As semi-aquatic amphibians, they've never conceived of flying."

"It is a thing in fiction stories, so actually we have thought of it. But no one takes it seriously! The thought of being up high in the air is terrifying, the stuff of nightmares. Ask any of our people." Sikall's large lavender eyes were widened to an extreme extent, and her breathing had increased dramatically.

The vehemence of her response was startling, and I wondered if the Dohannen really had an aversion to being up high, or if this was one of Sikall's personal issues. Certainly the top of the building we were in was quite high. From my studies of the Laldoralin Hegemony, most of the member worlds had developed air travel of one kind or another. Even spider-like Lieutenant Bitt-Nurr's people had lighter-than-air vehicles.

"Do you think there will be anything we can use here, Sikall?" Dr. Carstairs interjected, smoothly steering the conversation away from flying.

"There is a pause between each contest where people can… could…. eat. This required a lot of food on hand, and there's bound to be some of it that's capable of long-term storage, assuming no one else has pilfered it. We just have to find a place that provided the food and look for their storage."

Dr. Carstairs kept Sikall talking. You could tell from the trembly way she spoke (and the translator interpreted what she said) that the young Dohannen was very fragile emotionally, and my heart went out to her. I filed away what she said, but let the doctor do the talking. I couldn't imagine what it must've been like to see your species being hunted to extinction.

We came to the huge center pool, and I took a scan. The water was fresh with a few chemical agents for keeping it pure and I sent the scans up to Dora to see if it was drinkable.

"This is well within safe limits for consumption," she replied. "Whatever these chemicals are that they use to sterilize the water are not going to cause damage to your party, Tanner. Eventually it might be prudent to take a course of probiotics to replace stomach and intestinal flora, but that need would be sometime down the road from now."

"Looks like water's not a problem, then." I said. "If we're conservative, we might be able to wash up too."

"There's a blessing," Carstairs said. "I'm not used to smelling this bad."

"Look! This place will surely have still-edible food," Sikall said, running ahead to what looked like an eatery. A counter sat in an inset in the wall and a small wall surrounded a grouping of uncomfortable-looking chairs with tables. Above the counter, a sign appeared with a Dohannen looking benevolently down on us while what looked like various foods dotted the periphery of the signage.

It appeared so close to human culture that I had to look at Sikall to make sure there was no zipper on her skin to hide that we were being pranked by fellow Terrans.

Sikall jumped and slid over the counter and into a room in the back. She did something to the door along the wall, and it irised into the open position. Needless to say, my engineering suit wasn't going through a door that small, so I gestured Dr. Carstairs forward with as gentlemanly a flourish as a half-ton of armor allowed.

"Such good manners for a gear-head," she said, smiling. "Let's see if our little Sikall has found the answers to our supply problem."

Sikall had done just that. She emerged with several colorful pack-ages. "There's a lot here," she said. "The cold items are no good, but most of this, even if it's a little stale is still edible. At least by my people."

"Ensign Voss, why don't I stick here with Sikall and send scans of these foodstuffs to Dora for verification that it's human-compatible. You can continue reconnoitering the building."

"Sounds like a plan, Doctor. I'll see you back at Minnie."

I continued down the corridor, looking for another stairwell. Commander Torvald had said to look for a high vantage point, and I assumed that would either be the top floor or the roof if I could manage it. There were no signs of battle that I'd seen so far. At the end of one of the main passageway, I found a wide, spiraling ramp that went up to the next level. The Dohannen liked things smooth and flowing, not blocky and sharp. This seemed to extend to stair-ways too, which was convenient for me in my Mark II.

"Tanner," Dora said from my interior speaker. "I am now reading a new life form very near to your position. I do not know how it eluded my latest scanning of the structure."

"Is it new? Did someone slip past our perimeter?"

"Unlikely as the person nearing your position, a Dohannen, would have been seen easily from where I am. They must've been using stealth tech or been inside some sort of unscannable enclosure. They are VERY near to you."

Tunk.

I barely heard the noise, but realized it had come from behind me. I turned my head ninety degrees port, which was as far as my helmet would turn, but saw no one.

Tunk.

I saw the slightest of energy flares coming from my suit's shields and I realized that the tunk sound was coming from someone hitting my armor. Turning my entire body I was confronted with a very small Dohannen and from the wrinkles in his skin, a very old one. He was holding a metal bar of some kind, and as I looked at him, he hit my armor once more.

"Excuse me, old timer." I said. "I'd appreciate if you'd stop that. If you scratch the paint, I'm going to lose my deposit."

His eyes, which had been mismatchedly squinted, opened wide with astonishment as the matrix translated my words. "You… you're not Ravrath!"

"No, we are strange visitors from another world, and we're stuck here with you in the middle of your war. I'm going to open my helmet's face shield to show you what I look like. I'd appreciate if you could keep from screaming, and if you would, avoid hitting me with that bar again. You ready?"

"I guess I am. Let's see what sort of monster you are." He said.

"All right, here I go." I flexed a certain muscle, looked at a certain icon, and my face shield rose up. "What do you think?"

One eye squinted, then the other. "Hideous, but not as bad as the Rath in my book. So what in the deep cold are you doin' here? And how do you know our language?"

"You know that gate thing, out on the plain? Came through it from the far future. Trying to figure out a way to get back and take the rest of your kind with us. We've also developed a very good translation program."

He turned around a complete three-sixty, as if trying to find something in the surroundings of the sports arena. "I must've finally ate somethin' gone bad in the food left here. I'm probably dying, and you're just some sort of fever dream, aren't you? This is too insane t' be real."

I sympathized. I wanted very much to wake up in my bunk back on the *Seeker*, but I knew it wasn't going to happen. I reached out, and as gently as I could, pushed his shoulder. I should've know better than to try it in my Mark II. He went flying.

"Ow! Flappin' fins of Frang! What're you trying to do to me? I'm old!"

My guess was that my chances of being chosen for *Seeker's* first contact team if we made it back were pretty low now. "Sorry! Sorry. I didn't mean to do that, but my suit is a lot stronger than I thought and a lot less sensitive. But I bet you believe I'm real now, don't you?"

"Well I guess I do now," he said, rising from the floor and rubbing his shoulder. "So what are you doing in my hideout?"

"Seemed like a good place to hide from the fish people." I said. "Are you here alone? Our scans of the place didn't detect anyone here."

"It's just me. I been sleeping in the vault on the level below this in the offices. It's vented and you can open it from the inside so I figured it was the safest place in the building. What're you doin' wandering around in that giant suit?"

"I'm trying to find my way to the roof to set up an observation post. Can you show me how to get up there?"

He considered me a few moments then apparently made his decision.

"I'm still not convinced you're not a fever dream, but come with me, strange beastie. There's only one ramp to the roof."

◆

A few minutes later, we were at the top of the building. We could see the ocean from the top of the fin-shaped edifice we'd chosen. The old Dohannen leaned against a railing and sighed heavily.

"You got a name, Space Beast?" He asked.

"My name is Tanner. How about you?"

"I'm Krell. However you got here Tanner, you probably should go back where you came from. Staying around here to watch a civilization die seems like a terrible way to use your time."

"We're working on a way to get the gate to reverse itself. We want to take your people with us, the survivors at least," I said.

"This is a beautiful world," he said, "I hate the thought of leaving it to the Rav."

"It's still a beautiful world, even a half million years in the future. But in that time, there is no trace of your people, or the Ravrath. Our ship came here… um… then, to look at this planet as a possible colony site."

He turned half way towards me, giving me the side eye. "Well, Beastie, if you by some incredible stretch of fortune managed to get the remainder of our people into the future with you, won't that put sand in your finely crafted plans for takin' over the world?"

I shrugged, then realized that not only could he not see me do that in my Mark II, he probably wouldn't know what it meant if he could see it.

"Krell, that is above my pay grade. But I'm pretty sure, if we can get the Dohannen who are still alive back through the gate, my Captain will do everything in her power to aid you. Our scientists, Commander Torvald and Ensign Darkfeather are working with a Dohannen named Givall to try to figure out how to make it happen."

"They down there where you all set up?" he asked.

"Yeah. A couple of your scientists, some others and some kids. Contrary to what you said about yourself earlier, you seem pretty stable. Several of the others not so much. Maybe you could go down there and… I dunno… help them hold it together? Or talk to the kids."

"You mean do something useful, besides hiding?"

"I didn't mean it like that," I said. "But if there was ever a time to be a calming influence, this would be it."

The old amphibian looked toward the distant ocean. His eyes were seeing far away, but at someplace within, someplace traumatic. I'd seen the same look in all the Dohannen at one time or another, even the children.

"Yeah. Maybe I can cheer someone up, and maybe that will cheer me up." The old one turned and went back to the door we'd exited through. As it irised open, he turned and looked back at me. "I sure hope you're not a fever dream, Space Beast Tanner. This is the first time I've even felt an ember of hope in the last few years."

Chapter Fourteen

The next morning, Commander Torvald called a meeting of our team. I was finally out of my armor again and it felt good as we listened to the commander's progress report.

"I and Ensign Darkfeather," he said, " have been working with Givall and Lalall on the theory of the "Shelar" device. The two biggest hurdles are literally time and space. The device was intended as a last ditch effort, using very theoretical quantum entanglement science, to move remaining segments of the Dohannen population to colony worlds that would match their needs."

"We did receive a positive response from two of our attempts," Givall said. "The other attempt did not provide a response after they went through the Shelar. From what you've presented us, we know at least one of the attempts, the last one, went awry, causing the... deaths... of all involved."

"Do we know that the gate actually traveled through time," Dr. Carsairs said, "or has it just sat on the second moon for five hundred thousand years?"

"Unfortunately," Darkfeather answered, "from the scans that Dora took before we came through, there were a lot of bones buried under the surface of that moon. The high degree of acids and sulphur would've reduced them to dust had they been there more than ten years. The gate definitely emerged into our era."

We all paused to take that in. Those of us from the future knew that even if the refugees had come into our time right under the *Seeker's* nose, there's no way we could have gotten aid to them in time on that harsh and unforgiving planetoid. The Dohannen present with us all looked toward the ceiling, grief etched on their faces that not even alien biology could hide.

"So," Chief Moreland said, "do we have any chance at all of returning to our own time? Gotta say I'm not a fan of where we are now."

"We need three things," Torvald replied. "We need a larger power source than Minnie…"

"Why is that?" Carstairs asked. "She got us here, why is the miner insufficient to return us to the future?"

"The gate on the other end still had a charge left, from what Givall tells me. That's why it was able to draw the rest of what it needed from our machine. The gate here is completely discharged of all energy because our arrival drained the last of its power. The lines from the power plant the Dohannen used have been severed by the Ravrath. Evidently they understand that the gate is a method that their prey might use to escape them, though they might not understand exactly how."

"This is why," Lalall said, "when our previous groups arrived on the colony worlds they were supposed to access the protocol was to contact us, then initiate a destruct sequence to render the gate at their end unusable. We wanted to be sure that the Ravrath would have no opportunity to follow the colonists."

"It's quite obvious why that didn't happen to the gate you came here through," Givall added.

"Seems like maybe you should've all gone through that first gate," Chief Moreland said.

"We were worried that we would be putting all our fish in one tide pool," Lalall said. "Just because the colonists made it, did not necessarily mean that the colony world would be viable. Anything could happen. A contaminate, a voracious predator, an unstable star. We decided diversification would be the best path. In hindsight, I think we erred."

"Continuing, the second thing we need," Torvald interjected, "is to make contact with the forted-up Dohannen at the Citadel. If we make this work, we want to take as many of these people with us as we can. But, we're going to need someone to accompany whoever goes there, one of you.' He pointed to the amphibs.

"Why one of us?" The male Dohannen Datt asked. "You're the ones with all those armored suits."

"Just imagine your Citadel's defenders," I said, "looking out over the land for threats to the people they're defending. Just then, three aliens in massive power suits come strolling up to say hello. What kind of response do you think we'd get, Datt?"

"Henh, they'd hit you with everything they had," Krell said.

"Precisely," Torvald replied. "We need someone along to inform your people that we're not a new form of rapacious danger intent on destroying them."

"I will lead our new allies to the citadel," Givall said. "I know some of the people in charge there and hopefully we can gain entrance quickly."

"Bad idea," Darkfeather said. "You and Lalall are the only to experts we know of regarding gate travel. It needs to be one of the others."

"I'm not leaving this building," Datt said. "Between the fountains and the pools, we've got water and food for half an orbit. I'm not risking my dorsal nubs for this craziness. Time travel for Frang's sake!"

"I'll go," Sikall said. "Though I don't know the way."

"Like mud, you will," Krell said. "Be a cold day in a volcano before I let some child go traipsing into danger in front of me."

"I'm not a child! I've seen fifteen orbits!"

"And I've seen a hundred and ten orbits," the old Dohannen replied. "Was part of our military until I got too old. And I was stationed at the Citadel for a number of those years. Always wanted to go see it again."

"I think Krell would be the best choice," I said. "If he can make the trip all right."

"I can make the trip better than you, young space beastie, even without a fancy suit to carry me along like a tiny baby child."

"Hey, my ancestors evolved on land," I retorted, though to be true, I wasn't one hundred percent sure where the Laldoralin side had evolved from. "I'm pretty sure I could keep up, suit or no suit. Carry you, if I have to."

"Let's not be obnoxious to the people we're trying to help, Cadet," Dr. Carstairs said.

"If Krell is willing to make the journey for us," Givall interrupted, "then, assuming he can get the military there at the Citadel to listen, I can record a message that will tell them of our plan and a private bandwidth we can link communications together if they can get power to the underground media cables."

"Is the power to the gate carried by underground cables?" Ensign Darkfeather asked.

"Yes. Though we started the project ten-spans of orbits ago as a way to explore the stars we might like to colonize, the attacks by the Rav threw the entire endeavor onto a fast track. Nothing motivates our people and especially our leaders quite so well as being annihilated. Unfortunately, the power generation units were captured by the enemy."

"Add that to our list of things to overcome," Torvald said. "We either liberate those units or find an alternate source of power."

"Commander," I said. "You originally mentioned three things. Aside from power needs, what was the third?'

"We need to be able to recreate the conditions that took the gate into the future. That's where Dora comes in. I mentioned before how fortunate that we were that she's back in this time with us. She believes that with her sensor logs on Remora 2, she can give us the data we'll need to get this done."

"The sheer difficulty of computing such a complex problem with an almost infinite number of variables," Lalal said, "would take a super computer far beyond anything on this world."

"Let me tell you a little bit about the Laldoralin and their AIs," Torvald said. "The Laldoralin are one of the old races of this part of the galaxy. They specialize in "lifting up" younger races technologically and bringing them into the Hegemony, a confederation of systems."

"They kept us, the humans, from destroying our world and ourselves," Ensign Teo interjected.

"Yes" Torvald continued. "They are very technologically advanced, far beyond anything our people have come up with, even with them sharing technology. One of their most amazing creations, are their artificial intelligence constructs. Dora, whom you've heard through our speakers, off and on, is one of these hyper-intelligent computing systems. She makes the computers on our vessel, some of the best our planet Earth have ever created, look like toddler toys."

"More like neanderthal baby toys," Dora's voice emerged from the miner's exterior speakers.

"Did we mention," I said, "that Laldoralin AIs can also be pretty egotistical?"

"Tanner!" Dora objected.

"Hold on," Givall said. "You're telling me that this artificial intelligence is sentient?"

"I most certainly am," Dora said. "As sentient as anyone here, and perhaps even be more so. I assure you, with proper stimulation of your upper atmosphere using tools this Remora frame carries, I can recreate the needed solar interference to within one hundred thousand decimal points above the portal."

"Did these Laldoralin give this sentient to you," Lalall asked, "so that you could finish your human quest of exploration?"

Dead silence for a moment, then Torvald spoke. "Actually, if you wanted proof she's a sentient, she stowed away in our Remora probe so that she could keep an eye on him, her son." He pointed at me.

"What?" Givall said.

"Oh this is too much to..." Datt growled.

"Yer maman's a computer?" Krell asked.

The discussion dissolved into more loud queries and shouting until Chief Moreland cranked the volume on his suit and shouted, "That's enough! None of that is important and you can ask these questions if we're successful in surviving." He dropped the volume. "Right now, we need to decide which assets and resources are going into which jobs. I volunteer to escort ol' Krell here to the military base."

"Negative Chief," Torvald said. "I'm going to need you and Ensign Teo to scout the power plant. If there are too many Ravrath to engage, you pull back here. If there are a token group there that you feel the two of you can take, we need to get that power back."

"I'll go with Krell," I said.

"Sir," Moreland said, "you can't send the kid by himself."

"I understand your concerns, Chief, but I will reiterate my previous statement concerning Tanner's combat scores. With his sixth sense, I'm a lot less worried about him than I am about you and Ensign Teo."

Chapter Fifteen

We were originally going to wait for darkness, but the Dohannen with us told us that the Ravrath could actually see better in darkness. They insisted that strong daylight would actually be a better time to go. The Ravrath tended to stay out in the sun only as long as they had to, even when wearing full solar protection overlays on their helmets. Overlays I'd be more than happy to tear off their bodies.

Have some sunburn, slime bags.

Krell and I were moving just after dawn, the sun rising like a golden orb over a stunning distant ocean, pinkish-orange clouds above us. The delay had given everyone time to get a good rest.

"So damn stange to see Kaniber like this," the old one said. "I used to love walking this street, seeing the people and drinking a warm one. Old people making the best of their years, young ones being young, feisty and reproductive, trying to attract mates."

"Kaniber. That's this city, right?"

"Yes. One of many. One of many that are all like this, deserted. Frang-cursed Ravs." The old Dohannen said. "Thought we'd finally gotten far enough outside of each other's territories to have peace. Four hundred orbits ago, they got the oceans, we were stuck with the land. I'd love to swim the oceans again, but they drove us out. But we survived! We survived and we thrived."

"Oh. Them driving you out, that's awful, especially for a race like yours that came from the oceans."

"Yeah, Baby Beast, it is. This gate thing the scientists came up with seemed like it might be the answer. Go to another world leave the cursed frellers behind. But from what you told us, that didn't work either. Probably all them other colonists wound up in the heart of a star or deep space at the other end."

"Actually, Krell," Dora's voice came over my speakers, "that we are here, proves that the technology has worked, though obviously, more trials would have produced more reliable results."

"Well, I suppose that's good to know, if you say you can actually recreate the whole thing."

"There is one other thing, that I have only just informed the Commander and the rest of our group about. Two thing's actually."

"My ears 'r clear, AI lady. Let's hear 'em." A funny thing to say since Krell's ears were only two holes along the side of his head.

"I have finally had enough time to analyze genetic samples from your people. Dr. Carstairs sent me scans while providing first aid to your group. I can say with complete certainty that one of your colonies has become a thriving civilization in our time."

'The Medigans?" I asked.

"Indeed, Tanner," Dora said. "One of the earlier members of the Laldoralin Hegemony and one of our few amphibian members. They exist on a beautiful ocean world and are a very advanced species. My research work confirms that the Dohannen are the forebears of the Medigan. There is some genetic drift, but our time is over five hundred thousand orbits in the future."

Krell stopped short. "So, no matter what happens here, our species lives on, even if'n they're way far away."

"That is correct. I have also been granted access to the data on your colony gate coordinates. Accounting for stellar drift, Mediga is definitely one of the worlds that received one of your colonies. Even with the incredible distance, there can be no doubt."

The old Dohannen stopped and squatted, his hand gripping the sides of his head. Tears filled his over-large eyes.

"Thank you," he said. "Now at least we know that if the Ravs wipe us all out tomorrow, our people will continue. I'm not scared of dyin' but I was living in a kind of horrified state, terribly depressed, thinking that this was the end of us all. You gave me a gift I don't know if I can ever repay."

◆

The trek through the country side was fairly uneventful. While it's not that easy to move covertly in heavy engineering armor, we kept off the main roads and paths. We also had overwatch from on high with Dora helping us vector away from any Ravrath patrols.

"Tanner," Dora said. "You have several miles ahead with intensified Ravrath activity. I have charted a path that should allow you to avoid interaction with them. An indicator should be visible on your HUD, simply keep it centered on your display and you'll be on the path."

"Copy that," I said. "Krell, Dora's got a route laid out for us that should keep us mostly Rav free. How far is this installation?"

"About twenty five dards, Space Guppy."

"You know, you can just call me Tanner." A second later, a message on my HUD translated a dard into 1.31 miles. I hoped Dora would be direct-translating distances afterward.

"You think your military people will listen?" I asked. "I mean, we're basically talking about traveling through time. Back on my world, in the time I was born in, if a new idea was introduced, half the population would instantly call it a lie."

"Sounds like sentient life across the galaxy has a lot in common then," Krill replied. "Thing is, when you're being hunted and fed to some giant monster, you get a lot more open to any idea that might keep you alive. I have a feeling that our remaining leaders are ready to grasp any wave that might carry us to shore."

"That'd be great. With enough help, I'm betting between Givall, Commander Torvald and Dora we can pull this off, and save everyone."

"The optimism of youth. I hope you're right, Guppy."

"Forgive the interruption, son," Dora said. "But you seem to have picked up a tail."

I turned, and looked at our back-trail and noted that while Krell's tracks were barely visible, my own engineering suit-enhanced foot prints stood out starkly on the landscape.

'Who've we got, Dora? Rav patrol?' I'd had my suit speakers on to talk with Krell and he grew wary at my words.

"Negative. Life sign is Dohannen, and vector puts them following your trail. Perhaps a new straggler to rescue?"

"Let's be cautious anyway, Guppy," Krell said. "Move your big suited self across these rocks into that thicket of pophyr," He pointed to a thicket of purple and red brush. "In these days, I like to see who's following me before they see me."

We pulled off out of sight, with me stepping cautiously from stone to stone. Hopefully, members of a species that had left the ocean only five hundred years before wouldn't have developed into great trackers.

We sat there in the purple succulent brush and waited. Roughly five minutes later, a petite figure appeared, intently following my massive footprints. As it approached closer, I noticed a decorative tattoo on the side of her neck.

"Sikall! What are you doing?"

She started at my speaker-enhanced voice but seeing Krell and I, she walked over to us, the picture of guilty contrition. I don't know how well I displayed irritated astonishment through my visor, but Krell more than made up any lack. The older Dohannen was furious.

"For the love of Frang's fins! What do you think you are doing, young one? You were at least a bit safe where we left you. Why in the name of the great ocean would you come out here, following us?"

"I'm sorry, I had to follow you. I don't know any of those people back there! I want to go where everyone is hiding out to see if any of my friends or maybe even my parents are still alive," She stopped and looked at us with large limpid eyes that no human could've matched. 'Please, let me come with you. I won't get in the way."

"I'm more worried about you getting us caught," Krell said. "Well, Guppy what do you think?"

"Oh, good God," I said. "I guess we've come far enough it'd be more dangerous for her to try to find her way back. At least if she's with us we might, and I stress might, be able to protect her."

Sikall smiled with all the joy of one who'd put something over on everyone else.

◆

We knew we were getting close to where we were going by the number of bodies lying about. All of them Ravrath. Oddly enough, there were very few of their weapons there, with the exception of the occasional broken ones. Someone had taken them, and I wondered if it was the Rav or the Dohannen.

Less than a half mile from where we found the first bodies, we found wrecked tank-like machines. They looked formidable and had a series of what looked like cannons mounted on their front ends, From their appearance, I assumed these used the same water projectile technology of the Ravrath lances, only on a larger scale. Most of the tanks had holes in them that from the melted metal looked like the product of energy weapons. The number of bodies increased also. All Ravs.

"There it is," Krell said. Ahead was a huge metal wall, set into a mountain. It wasn't a wall in the traditional castle sense, there was no opening in the top. He continued: "Complex goes for miles into that mountain…"

Suddenly the wail of sirens blared across the countryside. Panels slid back and what could only be some sort of cannons moved forward, tracking to one single point before them.

In other words, they were all aimed at me.

Chapter Sixteen

A command blared over loudspeakers, loud enough that it took another half second for my suit to translate.

"Prepare to fire!"

"Holy crap!" I said. "I'm about to die."

I could see the cannons had all locked onto me and I assumed anything that could stop one of the Rav tanks would probably get through my shield and suit with no trouble.

"Don't shoot you reactionary fools!" Krell yelled, jumping in front of me. A few seconds later, Sikall joined him. I'm sure it looked ridiculous the two small Dohannen shielding me and my gargantuan armored form, but there we were.

"It has hostages!" The speakers blared. "Hold fire!"

"Guppy," Krell said, "Can you put my voice on your eternal speakers."

Yeah. One moment and... external mike and speakers are synched."

"Listen here, you stupid frangers!" Krell's voice boomed out of my suit, "My name's Krell, one-time member of the 2nd Tanolia (not translated). This here creature is not one of the Rav, he's a friend from an OFF-WORLD species! Understand? We need to talk to the people in charge if we're going to save Dohannen-kind. We're not going to get many more chances."

Silence from the shield-wall. A minute later, the panels with the energy weapons slid shut and a large double door at the base of the wall began to open. It slid to about a quarter of it's width, then stopped.

"Well," Krell said, "looks like we aren't going to be vaporized today."

"The day is still young," I told him.

"Don't worry, Tanner," Sikall said, "it'll be all right. We'll protect you."

"Thank you, Sikall," I said from behind my three inches of magna-shielded armor plating.

We started to move forward, and a group of Dohannen emerged, all in helmets and what looked like body armor of some sort. They carried short rifles that from the emitters looked like smaller versions of the mountain's defense weapons. Some of them carried Rav lances. They all looked hostile.

"Don't twitch a fin," one of them, a female warrior said. "What is this all about?"

"Me, the girl, and this one," Krell said, "have come to get things in order to get that portal thingie working again. We've got scientists back at the Event Palace in Kaniber. We need to talk to whoever's in charge. This might be our only chance to get whatever survivors of our species remain out of this mess."

"There's no way to power the portal," the warrior said. "The Ravs blew the lines from the power station."

"In one spot," Krell said. "Probably less than a days work to fix."

"In open country, with the Rav patrolling looking for groups to lead to slaughter," the warrior replied.

"Are you in charge here?" I asked. The soldiers stepped back. The behemoth hath spoke and they didn't know what to make of it. No one said a word. "I am sorry to have to say this, it's an old cliché about aliens on my world, but… take me to your leader."

"You heard the weird metal giant," Krell said. "Let's get in there."

The one who'd spoken before gestured to follow and started toward the opening. I assumed that she was the equivalent to the captain of the guard and they were going to give us a chance to plead our case. We followed.

Once we were through, the massive gate began to close behind us. The captain stopped in front of me.

"Are you able to function outside that suit of armor?" she asked pointedly.

"Uh… yes I can. My species is compatible with your atmosphere."

"Probably came here to steal our planet," another guard said. I might've been more offended, but I'd read all of the accounts of humanity's behavior during the time I'd been sleeping in cryo, during the Laladoralin's "first contact" year. Our reaction was the same as his, multiplied to a factor of one hundred. It'd been fortunate that the Laldoralin's defense capabilities were far in advance of our weapons at the time.

"As far as I'm concerned," Sikall chimed in, "he can have the frelling planet, as long as he blasts the Ravs to small bloody pieces."

"Language, Young One," The captain said in a mild tone. "Alien person, if you want to get near our leaders, you're going to have to vacate that armor. There's no way you're getting close to them in that thing."

"Don't do it son," Dora said over my internal speakers, "you'd be defenseless. I don't want you to place yourself in danger."

Switching to internal speakers I replied; "I have to, Mom. If we can't trust these people, we're gonna likely be toast anyway. Please lock down my suit as soon as I exit."

"I will. But if they hurt you…"

"It'll be okay."

I hit the release that swung the back of my suit open and backed out. The air smelled sweet compared to the recycled oxygen I'd been breathing. As soon as I was clear, a couple of the guards tried to crowd in to get a look at the armor's interior. They were disappointed when in closed itself up and locked down.

"Wow," one of the guards said, giving me the once-over, "It looks a little weird, but I thought it'd be more… alien. Like maybe have tentacles and twenty eyes." My sub-dermal implant, a micro computer by itself provided the translation. The speaker on the padd at my hip translated for the Dohannen.

"That's enough, Grennel," The captain said. "You, strange one, come with me. All three of you."

We were fast-marched farther into the complex, and passed many soldiers, all sitting in various states of readiness, some alert, some sleeping and many sitting against walls staring off into space. I couldn't say for sure, but I guessed many of them were looking into their own private versions of hell. You can't survive the genocide of most of your species without having scars, inner and outer.

As we got farther in, the press of soldiers gave way to hordes of what could only be civilians. Children ran past, chasing each other, but the adults mostly looked like they'd given up. Like they'd come to the conclusion that it was only a matter of time before they and their progeny were rounded up and fed to a giant sea monster.

These people need a giant infusion of hope.

We went down and down into a large cavern system interspersed with armored sections and high tech stations that were most likely security-based. At last, we came to a series of metal doors that led to elevators. The doors were iris-openings, and stopped in mid-slide, then started again, then finally opened like an old camera shutter to let us in the elevators. I had a suspicion that they were supposed to operate much more smoothly than they did.

Once in, we descended, then descended some more. When we emerged, we were a couple hundred feet below the cave, and to one side there was a body of water. I didn't smell an 'ocean smell' and assumed it was fresh, probably supplying the needs of the people above.

"This place is our last ditch fall back government center," Krell told me. "We've mistrusted the fish-faces since we were forced from the ocean, peace agreements aside. We just never thought they'd go this far."

"They might not have," I said, "if their tails hadn't been on the line."

"I guess they decided desparate times called for desparate measures," Krell replied. "Not that I've ever thought they'd be upset if we went extinct."

'We're here," the captain said. "Our leaders will be in momentarily to speak with you."

We were led to a wide oval-shaped room and the captain gestured for us to sit. That was fine for Krell and Sikall, but the slope-backed chair wasn't easy for me to get comfortable in. I finally wound up sitting on the edge, trying to keep my spine upright. Moments later, three Dohannen came in through a side door. Each of them were dressed in shiny, silky-looking garments, almost like the saris of India back on Earth. They oozed with the feeling of authority. Their composure was interrupted however, once they got a look at me.

"They said that we had an alien visitor, but…" a very tall female said. "You… you are actually from another world." She sat down, none too gently, into one of the sloping chairs. "When I was told this… I could not believe it."

"I am Tanner Voss," I said, thinking that I should've brought Dr. Carstairs with me. "I am from the planet Earth starship, *U.S.S. Seeker*. I and my team mates wound up here as an accident when we found the last gate that you sent your colonists through."

"The colony that was aimed for the oceanic world farther in the galactic arm? Or the gate for the green world farther out toward the edge of this galaxy?" another one of the leaders asked.

"I'm guessing the latter," I said. "May I ask your names before we continue?"

All three leaders sat down, and the female who had first spoken gestured toward herself and said; "I am Tivonne, speaker of the Triumvirate. These are Dekell and Kivar, the last two remaining members of our house of government. All the others who led our people are… missing."

"I understand, thank you. If I am correct, my people came through the gate aimed outward on the spiral arm. From what we have gleaned, your gate to the water-world was successful and the colony there will become a thriving civilization."

I knew my phrasing seemed odd to them, and I waited for them to ask the reason for my surety. Instead, Dekell, the other female asked, "You are obviously a space-faring race. Can your planet of Earth come to our aid. Can they take our remaining population somewhere safe?"

"They cannot aid you," I said. "Our civilization does not exist yet."

All three Dohannen looked at me like I had suddenly spouted horns, an effect even more pronounced by the fact that they'd never even seen an alien of any kind before.

"Listen, to the young one," Krell interjected and I had to make sure he was talking about me and not Sikall, "he and his people and their gear are from the far future of this world. I have a recording from your chief gate scientist Givall…"

"Givall lives?" Tivonne said, standing abruptly.

"Yes, he and his wife are still alive and the recording explains all of this, so let's hear it, shall we?"

Tivonne returned to her seat and Krell placed the video padd that Commander Torvald had loaned Givall on the table. A few moments later, the holographic image of the scientist appeared above the device at about half of normal scale.

"Greetings to our leaders, those of you who may remain. I am Givall, who you most likely already know, or know of through my work on our world's escape gates. The young being who has accompanied our messenger, Krell, is one of a small number of alien allies who've come through the gate on the plain of Fillan. They have technology and knowledge that may help us reactivate the gate for one last chance opportunity to escape from the horror that has become our world."

I am so glad that Givall recorded this. I didn't want to be the one that had to explain this whole situation, especially the time-traveling aspects.

The message ran through smoothly up until the time when Givall told them about the misaligned gate and the thousands who had died on Hell.

"Pause it!" Dekell said, rising when I did so. "So what then? The gate kills tens of thousands, and he wants us to try it again?"

"From the future?" Kivar, the lone male leader said with no small amount of scorn. "You expect us to believe such nonsense. This alien is probably one of ours with extensive remake surgery and…"

"To what purpose?" Krell roared, surprising the hell out of all three bureaucrats. "At this point, I'd be willing to accept help from ol' Trickfin himself! This is literally your and our last chance."

"We are safe here," Kivar said. "The Ravrath have not been able to breach the wall."

"Yet," Tivonne said. "They have not breached the wall yet."

"Listen people," I said. "My team and I are going to get back where and when we came from somehow. We'll do it with or without your help, but we wanted to try and take as many of you with us to the safety of the future. I assure you, all those hundred-orbits down the line, when my people first orbited this world, there was no sign of intelligent life, none. Not Dohannen, not Ravrath. Just an empty world."

"Please." Sikall said. "They are trying to help us. What do we have to lose by trusting them?"

◆

An hour after the three politicians said they needed to talk and left us, I was sitting more comfortably against the wall while we waited.

"We should've patched them in through comms to Givall and Commander Torvald. I botched this," I said. "They're just gonna do what they perceive as the safe thing and hunker in this bunker."

"Isn't on you, Guppy," Krell said. "These three are lifetime politicians. They always run for the safe harbor, thinking that inaction is safer than actually doing something. I wonder if they'll even tell the people here about this and take a vote."

"They have to, Krell," Sikall said. "I'm just a young one compared to them and even I can see that the food supply here will run out eventually. Staying here is a short-term solution."

"Well, maybe we're just being pessimistic," I said. "It could be we're reading their reactions wrong and they'll return on board with the whole idea."

"Didn't like their reactions, Guppy," Krell replied, giving a side eye look toward the door the politicians had exited. "Maybe it'll be okay, but I have an idea how to help ensure their cooperation. Sikall? I want you to take this," Krell handed the young woman the padd he'd brought. "Get as big a group together as you can out there and show them this. Guppy? Will this be translated?"

"Yes, it's set to automatically do so. The translation is only for my people anyway. Givall is one of you."

"Good. Sikall, take it and go. Show as many people as you can, and drop hints that it might not happen because these three aren't in the same sea with it. Spread the rumors among the military people too. Their dorsal's on the line same as everyone else."

"I'll do as you say, old one." Sikall rose and left the room.

"If our leaders get spineless, maybe the people can put some lava under their feet," Krell said, looking toward where the triumvirate had gone.

I took my own padd off my belt, paired with my sub-dermal transceiver and called Dora. "Mom? How are things with everyone else?" I hoped that the depth in the rock we were sitting at wouldn't occlude communications, but Dora answered clearly within seconds.

"Commander Torvald, Ensign Darkfeather and the Dohannen scientists continue to work on the calculations needed for our attempt to return through the gate. I am assisting remotely. Ensign Teo and Chief Moreland are returning from their reconnaissance of the power plant."

"How did that go?"

"Not well. My scans show that the Ravrath have it tightly locked down and Moreland agrees that it would take a full assault to get the power plant free of our enemy's influence. He is hoping that your negotiations are going well."

"It's not looking good," I admitted. "Their leaders did not seem enthused about doing anything that requires risk, even though their situation here can't last. I really wish I'd have brought Doc Carstairs. I feel kinda out of my depth here."

"I am sure that you are not giving yourself enough credit, Tanner.

Dr. Carstairs has been recording everything she can of Dohannen culture. She seems quite confident that we will return to the *Seeker* and she will become famous for her work with these people."

"I guess we'll see how that goes. If the leader won't play ball, Krell has a little plan to do an end run around them. Whether that will work is anyone's guess, but we plan to lay things out for the people if the leaders hide from responsibility."

"Please let me know what progress you make," Dora said, "so I can relay your imminent success to Commander Torvald."

"Will do, Mom." I cut the connection. I glanced at the padd's chronometer. We'd been waiting for over an hour and a half. A few moments later, the captain of the guard came in and gestured for us to follow her.

"The Triumvirate is taking longer than planned to come to a consensus," she said. "They want you to be comfortable while you wait and have had a room prepared for you to wait in. There is food, and more comfortable furniture for your strange body type."

She led us down a narrow hallway going deeper into the complex and showed us to a room with a table, some couches and chairs. A view screen adorned one wall and food was set out on the table.

As I sat on one of the couches, the captain deftly, with the skill of a pickpocket, slid my padd off my belt and hurried toward the door.

"Hey! What the hell are you doing?" I yelled, coming to my feet and starting after her.

"Oh, franging dung," Krell said.

She exited the room quickly and large see-through sliding doors came in from the side. They closed so fast that I barely avoided having my nose shortened. She turned, looked at me impassively and spoke.

"The Triumvirate has decided to deny your request, and at their order you are to be held here until they decide what to do with you. Food and water will be provided, and waste-product elimination is through the small door in back. I am sorry, but these are my orders."

"What's your name, Captain?" My sub-dermal implant was providing the translations now.

"I am Koabac," she replied, "I am the highest ranking officer left in our military. I regret that I must do this to you, Alien, but I have my orders."

"Your leaders don't want to help us, that's fine," I said, trying to keep my anger under control. "But just take me out to my suit and kick me out the front door. There's no need for this. As far as I'm concerned now, you can all sit here in these caves until you starve or the Rav break in. Let me go and we can be done with each other."

"Like the guppy says," Krell said, coming up beside me, "there's no need to incarcerate us."

"You were in the military?" She asked him.

"Yes."

"Then you know I'm not going to disobey orders. Again, sorry, but this is the way it is." Koabac turned on her heel and walked briskly away.

"Well," Krell said. "I truly didn't expect this."

"That's why we're in here, I guess."

Chapter Seventeen

When there's nothing you can do, fretting won't help. My 23rd century stepfather on Earth had drilled this into my sister and I. He told us to look for the most productive thing we could do in the interim.

So I slept.

I'd been burning the candle at both ends for several days now and the couches were indeed comfortable. Krell, however, couldn't stop stewing about our treatment. My ability to sit and wait without fretting didn't sit well with him either.

"How the hell can you sleep when we're losing valuable time, Guppy? These turd-slingers are supposed to lead the people and all they're doing is sitting on their dorsals while the frangin' Rav lead us toward extinction. At least those of us Dohannen that are still left on this planet."

My sub-dermal transceiver translated his words so fast that there was no lag. It also translated my words outward through my collar insignia/transmitter, and there was a slight lag that way. The collar transmitter was intended for shipboard messaging. The computing power came from the dermal implant.

"You were ex-military weren't you, oh Ancient Fart?" If he could keep calling me guppy, I could give a little back. It didn't seem to faze him in the least, though.

"Yeah, what about it? There's no one here in these soldiers I even recognize, so don't expect any loyalty or sympathy from them."

"You served here," I gestured toward the hallway. "You know any way of circumventing this door?"

"I was not an electronics expert, Guppy and these doors aren't the kind you pick with a piece of fish bone and a lip ring. How about you? Can you contact yer mama in the sky and see if she can help us?"

"Can't reach her. If I still had my padd, I could punch a signal through all this rock, but I've tried with my sub-dermal transponder, which I'd appreciate you not mentioning to anyone else, and it's just not strong enough."

"Koabac certainly called that one when she grabbed your device."

"If I had my suit, I could easily not only contact Dora, but break those doors as well. In about an hour though, I will miss my check-in with her and she'll start to get worried. Two hours after that when I miss another check in she'll know things went wrong. Though I'm not sure what she could do against a fortress of laser cannons and soldiers."

"Shame. Maybe she can get Givall to somehow convince them. Obviously we weren't persuasive enough."

"From the way I read this," I said, "and I admit you've got a lot more experience than me, but if Tivonne and the others got ahold of Givall and Lalall they'll probably throw them in here with us. Then we could all sit and stew until the Rav showed up to lead us to our dinner appointment."

The old one sighed. "Yea, I'd guess you're pretty well spot on with that. Most politicians for our people tend to do just enough to point to and never really try to move things forward."

"As you said once, must be something that crosses over in all species," I replied.

◆

Three hours later, things hadn't changed much. Krell had calmed down enough to take a nap, I snacked on the table food hoping that the compatibility with human digestive tracts applied to the food here too.

As I gazed idly out through the glassine doors, I noticed a furtive movement in the hallway. I stood up and went over to the clear surfaced door and waited. A moment later, Sikall appeared at the exterior, accompanied by one of the Dohannen soldiers, one I'd not seen before.

"Tanner," she said, pressing the intercom button, "I went back to the conference room and you were gone. This is my friend Geddle.

He checked up on you and found they'd locked you in here! What is happening?"

"Your leaders decided they didn't want to do anything useful and didn't want your people to get any ideas. Hence, Krell and I wound up locked in this back hallway."

Krell, now awakened, joined me at the door. "Were you able to show that projection around?"

"Yes, and you were right. Geddle and a number of the other soldiers are wondering why we're not doing something to make this happen right now."

"I left your device with a comrade of mine," Geddle said, "and he's showing it to all the civilians he can reach. It will hit a tipping point soon I think."

"Geddle," Krell said, "Can you get us out of here?"

"I can't. I don't have the access code. Only Captain Koabac has the codes for the cells, just in case there's a mutiny amongst the troops. She wants anyone she puts down here to be under her fins."

We were at an impasse. They couldn't get us out and we couldn't help convince anyone what the stakes were. Then, I had an idea.

"Sikall, can you get the padd back and call Dora? She'll be monitoring for it."

"I'm sure I can. What do you want me to tell her?"

"Is my suit still where I left it?"

"Yes, there's only one guard on it. Everyone knows you vacated it."

"Good," I said. "Here's what you and Geddle can do…"

◆

It was almost an hour later when I heard thuds coming down the corridor. A few moments later, Geddle appeared in front of our door, a weapon in his hand as if he was on patrol. A moment later my engineering suit appeared behind him. On his belt was the second padd with Givall's message stored on it.

"It went as you said, Tanner Voss," Geddle said. "I told everyone we'd gotten into your armor and were taking it deep into the mountain for study."

"Tanner?" Dora's voice came over my transceiver, "Do you read me?"

"Hi mom, good to hear your voice. Sorry to tell you, but I'm in jail."

"What every mother wants to hear," she replied. "Are you and Krell all right?"

Krell appeared at my side. "Who's driving that monster armor, Guppy? I wouldn't think anyone here'd have the knowhow to be piloting it."

"I am in control," Dora said. "If you will give me a moment, I will open that door for you. Please stand back."

"Try not to cause too much damage," Geddle said. "I'm in enough trouble as it is."

I thought she'd use the plasma cutter in the right arm, but Dora simply drove the armored gauntlets of the Mark II into the seam of the door and began to pull. A few seconds later, sparks and smoke flew from a panel near the door and the panels slid apart.

"I can hold the door for you," she said. "Unless I am ready to destroy the door completely I can't open it further. It keeps trying to re-close."

Krell started forward but I put my hand on his chest. "Wait a second. Krell, the only way I see this going is having to fight our way out. We might not make it, especially once we clear the gate. But more importantly, people are going to get hurt and that is the exact opposite of what we want to accomplish here. I don't want to be responsible for any Dohannen casualties."

The old one blew out a breath. "Yes. We came here to try an help and that sure won't help anyone. You thinking we need to let Sikall and Geddle try to win more people to our side?"

"Nobody needs us yet, if you really think about it. Lets put the suit over there in the corner where it can't be seen from the hall, and let our allies see if they can sort out a bloodless coup."

"You, Geddle," Krell said. "Take that padd back up and tell Sikall to keep trying to get support for our plan. It's not gonna do our people much good if the Guppy here escapes and he an his people leave us behind. You have to make this happen, soldier. Even if your superiors are in opposition. This is literally for the fate of all of us left on this planet."

Geddle sighed. "Yes. Standard procedure. Move rocks from Hole A to Point B. Why are those rocks not in Hole A? Move rocks back where they were. I'll start moving rocks."

"Good lad," Krell told him. "Go save the Dohannen race."

Chapter Eighteen

We waited and we waited. Several hours later, Krell had found a game board in one of the cabinets. He was trying to teach me to play this particular game called "Sreevo" without much luck. It wasn't that the game was too hard to learn, I just couldn't keep my mind focused on it.

I had checked in with Commander Torvald through my suit's tranceiver and told him about the challenges we were facing. He agreed we were pursuing the best course in trying to change hearts and minds in the military and civilian Dohannen.

Meanwhile, he and Darkfeather, in conjunction with Givall and Lalall, had finished the calculations for activating the portal and causing the glitch that moved it's destination through time. Dora had confirmed their findings and now the problems were all practical, how to power the device and get all of the remaining Dohannen to it then through it.

"Commander, I still see one big problem. One back in our time."

"Yes," he replied, "the destination gate's current location. There's only one thing to do about it, we're going to have to fire it up twice and send one of us through to contact *Seeker* and see if they can move it to the surface."

"I bet Dora could handle that, but she'd need to be shielded, sir."

"In looking at the calculations we've come up with, I don't think that would be possible. We just don't have what we need to give her that level of protection. It'll have to be one of us, in a Mark II, possibly with a secondary power source carried. Anyway, we'll keep working on ideas, you keep us posted on your situation."

"Aye, Commander."

We disconnected and Krell gestured toward the board again. I sat back down to see if I could get a handle on the game. Krell held up his hand.

"Guppy, listen."

Voices were in the hallway and getting louder. A few moments later, Koabac and three soldiers came around the corner, heading our way. I glanced to where the suit stood open and ready just out of sight, wondering just how fast I could get into it. My chances were good.

"Krell," Koabac called out.

"What's going on, Koabac?" Krell sneered. "Decided the guppy and I are too dangerous to keep alive?"

She stopped in mid-stride. I was no expert on Dohannen expressions, but the one on her face seemed to be offended.

"What?" she said. "Why would you say that? We're not monsters."

"Dunno about that. Our people have no hope of long-term survival and we show up with a chance for them to survive. Instead of listening and planning, you throw us in a cell. Sounds either monstrous or stupid to an amazing degree."

Koabac sighed. "I have to agree. Let's call it monstrously stupid on my part." She went to the wall panel and opened the door. "However, I've finally come to the conclusion that the Triumvirate's way will doom everyone. My soldiers will follow me, so effectively, you have won the argument."

"Good to hear," Krell. Told her. "How much of the populace is on board?"

"You must understand, old soldier, we're not going to save everyone."

"Why not?" I asked. "If we can get the gate going and everyone through it, this world in the future has no Ravrath."

"The problem, my alien friend, is that we won't get everyone through it. You may think I'm speaking of casualties, but what I mean is that not everyone will follow us from this sanctuary at the appropriate time. Some are like a zinrool in the tall kelp. Even when the karkeek sees them they will still freeze in place, praying they won't be found.

"We have to convince them," I said. "Surely we can sell everyone on survival."

"Guppy," Krell said, shaking his head, "you're young. You don't yet understand the power of fear mixed with temporary safety. I think we'll convince most, but there will be some you couldn't pry out of here with a mega-driver."

"If we could get the hold-outs to listen to me, I could 'sell' them on the idea."

"All right, young one. We'll see if you can get them to listen."

"We have another problem, though," Koabac interrupted. "Tivonne has come around to our way of thinking, but the other leaders, Dekell and Kivar are adamantly opposed to leaving the Citadel under any circumstances. They've locked myself, Tivonne and everyone else out of the gate controls and turret operations. They're in effect, holding us all prisoner here."

"Well." I said. "Pretty sure we can circumvent that."

"And just how will you do that?" She asked.

I walked over to the corner where my suit was standing just out of sight, climbed in and sealed it up. I walked over to where an astonished Koabac and her team stood."

"How did that get in here!?"

"Well, ma'am," I replied. "Let's just say that I and my people have always believed in being pro-active."

◆

Ten minutes later, suited up, I accompanied Krell, Koabac and her team to the main living area. I now towered above the others and when we hit the huge common area, everyone looked up with concern at my large armored form. How Geddle had managed to slow walk it down to us seemed like a bit of a miracle.

We were passing all the civilians when Tivonne, the only friendly member of the Triumvirate came striding up to us with her assistant.

"Greeting Krell and esteemed visitor," she said. "I greatly regret that we imprisoned you. I have had time to do some thinking, a great deal of thinking, and I acknowledge that your plan is the only plan to save everyone here."

"I take it," I said via suit speaker, "your two fellow Triumvirate members are not in agreement with you."

"I see news travels fast. Dekell and Kivar have locked down this installation. If any of us do attempt to breach the outer doors the defense weapons will fire on anything that moves. That includes the Rav, you and any of us."

"Damn fools!" Krell said. "They're doing this because they're cowardly Frang-turds. Bet they're saying this is for everyone's "own good" but they're just too afraid to take a chance."

"Whatever their reason," Koabac interjected, "They've sealed themselves into the administrative section and we don't dare blast our way in because that's where all the computers are that control this place. Lights, air, power, everything that keeps us going down here."

"Let me check in with my associate," I said. I keyed my tranceiver over to a private channel and killed my exterior speakers. "Mom? Do you copy."

"Yes, Tanner. How are things down there?"

"Kinda messed up. Two of the Dohannen leaders have holed-up in the admin. section of this place and put everyone into lockdown. Oh, and by the way, don't go anywhere near the entrance to this place. The aforementioned jackasses have set the place's defenses on autopilot. They'll blast anything that moves."

"Need some help?"

"Oh, all we can get, I'd say." I replied. "I can probably cut my way in, but the computers here run everything and if I damage them, conditions won't be pretty. Think you can hack in?"

"Please. I'm a Laldoralin Class One AI. I'm now in. That took all of a second. It's like working with tinker-toys."

"Yeah. As I remember, didn't you say something similar about the *Seeker's* computer system?"

"Now Tanner, I didn't mean to disparage your biological mother's people's technology, but let's be honest. Your father's people's technology, AKA me, is…"

"Thousands of years more advanced," I said. "Seems to me I've heard that more than once Mom."

"No need to be flippant, young man. I sometimes long for the days when I had a body and could ground you."

"Life moves on, Mom. We must accept that. Can you open those doors?"

"Consider it done, because it now is. Best tell our new friends."

"Thanks Mom. You're the best."

I switched back to exterior speakers, though I left the channel to Dora open. "The problem is solved, I believe. The doors should respond now."

"What?" Koabac said. "How?"

"Eye in the sky, Guppy?" Krell asked.

"Eye in the sky, Krell."

◆

The doors to the administrative section opened as if they'd never been locked. I, Koabac and three soldiers entered first, checking for anything fishy. No traps of any kind which wasn't a big surprise. Dekell and Kivar hadn't exactly struck me as the commando type.

"It's alright," Koabac called back to the assembled throng of people crowding the entrance. "Come in, but be careful."

Tivonne led the group in and they spread out looking for the two offending politicians. I was hoping there wasn't going to be some bloody frontier justice. I opened what looked like the computer room, and a skinny Dohannen inside took one look at me and screamed. I'm sure that the featureless face of my suit did little to reassure him.

"You the one that did Dekell and Kivar's dirty work, mate?" I asked.

"Frang! What are you?"

"I'm the space alien, Numbskull. I thought you were good at this, keep up!"

Our conversation was cut short when a group of angry civilians stormed in and dragged him out of his chair. A couple started landing blows on his head and I had to step forward and turn up the volume on my speakers.

"Hey!" I thundered. The volume started everyone, and lowering the volume I continued. "I understand you're angry, but we don't know this guy's story yet. Dekell and Kivar may be wankers," (I had no idea how that would translate) "but for all we know, this fellow could've been coerced. So let's save the vigilante justice until we know the whole story."

"They made me do it," Computer guy moaned. "They said if I didn't do what they said, my mate and our kids would have their rations cut off!"

Most of the Lynch mob backed off at that, though a few hard-core lads were still giving him the stank-eye. One muttered, "Yeah? Just how the hell were they going to pull that off? No one here would've let that happen."

Personally, having grown up in the 21st century, I thought the fellow's lack of belief in the politician's ability to screw the little guy was a bit naive. We were interrupted by a commotion in the main room. Looking back that way, I saw that a crowd had formed as the soldiers brought Dekell and Kivar out.

It was getting ugly fast. The Dohannen did not like their leaders pulling things like this, and the chance that they'd simply beat them to death seemed very real. Kivar already had one eye half-closed in the Dohannen equivalent of a black eye. Koabac and her soldiers formed a chain around the two.

"Everyone back away," Koabac yelled in a voice that would've done my combat instructors at the academy proud. "These two will stand trial by tribunal. There will be no vigilanteism here today. NOW BACK OFF!"

I was about to step forward to back her up, but the crowd did as she told them.

"The trial will be swift, I assure you all," Tivonne said. "I, Captain Koabac and... Krell will make final judgement here. Krell? Will you take the lead in this?"

The old soldier sighed. "Yeah. Let's get this done."

Judgement was swift. The tribunal quickly decided the fate of the two politicians. Even though several of the civilians wanted them executed, Kivar and Dekell were pronounced banished. A few minuted later, the doors to the Citadel were opening and they were being prodded outside. They weren't given any weapons or supplies.

It was the next best thing to being executed.

"Please," Dekell begged before being shoved out. "We made a mistake out of fear. Please have mercy!"

"You know, Krell," I said. "Your people are going to need every bit of genetic diversity you can muster if we get out of here. Maybe you could..."

"We'll do without their genes, Guppy. Thanks for your input," he said, with finality.

I shut up. Not my circus. But it was hard to see Dekell's tear-filled eyes pleading at us through the closing gate. Kivar was already shuffling toward the tree-line in the gait of a broken being.

Chapter Nineteen

Everyone was silent for a moment, then Tivonne turned to Krell and said; "We need to start formulating a plan, figure out our objectives and methods for accomplishing them."

"Seems to me, we have three main goals. Tell 'em Guppy," he said.

"Well, first thing we need is to retake the power plant," I said. "I'd defer to you and Captain Koabac on the best way to do that. Then we need to get the power going. Seems like the last thing might be the hardest, though. Moving all these people to the gate and holding position there until we can get a stable wormhole."

"Oh," I paused a moment on how to word my next statement, "and one of my people in one of these suits, will need to go through to the future and get my Captain there to use the *Seeker* to move the gate down to the planetary surface."

"Oh," Tivonne said. "Is that… all."

"Madame, it sounds impossible," Koabac said. "But only if you take it as one great group of tasks. Break it down into smaller tasks and I assure you, if the science works, the military forces under your command will make it happen."

"Were it not for you and the military," Tivonne replied, "I think our people would be extinct at this point. You have held the line against impossible odds to give these people a fighting chance at survival."

It was about this time that I noticed one of her staff members holding up what looked suspiciously like a recording device. I guessed that this little mini-speech was going out to the population of the Citadel via the many numerous screens that were placed everywhere.

"From what our alien visitor tells us, one of the gate colony attempts was successful, and in the far future becomes a thriving civilization. Is this not so, Visitor?"

The ball was in my court. I'd said that I wanted a chance to convince everyone to leave the Citadel when the time came and now was my chance. I think my heart rate may have doubled in that moment.

Please don't let me screw this up.

"Your descendants are called the Medegin," I said, "and they inhabit a watery planet many light-years from this world. They are a thriving civilization, far ahead of my own, and were one of the species that helped uplift mine. They, and others, prevented us from destroying ourselves and our world. My people, the people of the planet Earth, owe them a debt that is difficult to repay. I would very much like to help you all to get out of the situation we're in now. I assure you, the future is bright if we succeed."

"Well said," Tivonne replied, the camera worker turning back to her, "the off worlders have given us a last chance. I have not wanted to point this out in this seemingly hopeless time but we, the remaining Dohannen on this world, are running out of options. Captain Koabac, how stand our supplies for our people's long-term survival?"

Conscious that she was being video broadcast, the tough security leader seemed almost reticent. "I'm afraid I know that without looking, Madame Speaker. Going as we have, we will run out of food within three telps."

I glanced at the small window of my HUD to look for the translation of the timing. About four months.

"We can go a bit longer with severe rationing," Koabac continued, "but the time that we can hide behind these walls is rapidly coming to a close. Then we will have to venture back to our cities to try and forage what we can."

'Which is a losing game, long-term," Tivonnne interjected. "We may last a few more months, at the cost of being picked off person by person as we try to find food. To put it bluntly, we need a solution. The gateway is our last hope. No one will be forced to leave the Citadel, but we won't be leaving much in the way of supplies behind."

She'd decided to play hardball. Without the Citadel's supplies, anyone who stayed would have to leave eventually. But I saw where she was coming from. If by some miracle we pulled this off and sent all these people to the future, we'd have a population raised in a technological society dumped onto what would be in essence a wild planet. They'd need every supply they could take.

The Seeker and her crew would offer all the aid we could, but one ship could only do so much for upwards of twenty thousand refugees.

Tivonne turned and looked directly into the video feed. "We are still creating our plan to make this work and I want to keep everyone in the loop. Ideas will be very welcome. We may not be able to implement all of them, but any idea that might help us make this happen will be considered."

It was inspiring stuff. But we all new this was a last ditch effort and I sincerely hoped desperation would become the mother of invention. We had some of the Seeker's best back at the events palace, but it was going to take some damn good ideas to accomplish our goals, and some of them would have to come from the Citadel.

I moved a ways off from the crowd and called Dora. "Mom, do you copy?"

"Yes, Tanner. I hope you don't mind, but I am monitoring what is happening down there through your suit. I felt it would be in all our interests to have live updates."

"No argument here," I said. "Will you update the commander, or should I?"

"I think it would be best if you spoke with Commander Torvald directly. He may wish to give you new orders."

"Roger that, will you connect me?"

"You are connected."

"Tanner?" Torvald's voice came over my speakers. "Status report."

"Sir, reason has prevailed at the Citadel, though there has been some house-cleaning. The leader of the Dohannen here is named Tivonne, and she's embraced the "get off this world" protocol wholeheartedly." I spent a few minutes giving my superior officer a play by play of everything that had transpired. "So, it looks like we are green for the next phase, sir."

"I am very glad to hear it. Cadet, I have new orders for you. I need for you to return to our location and retrieve Ensign Darkfeather and Dr. Carstairs. They will act as liaison with the people of the Citadel. Darkfeather will also be better suited to help their tech people and military coordinate the strikes and takeovers we need to engage in."

"Relieved to hear it, sir," I told him. "I was feeling a bit out of my depth, and am quite ready to hand those duties off."

"I thought you might be. You still have several hours of daylight left, so start out ASAP. You can make the return trip tomorrow. Make sure to let the Dohannen know you're going, too."

"Understood, sir. Anything else?"

"Just be very cautious and try not to get jumped. Torvald out."

◆

After explaining the situation to Krell and Koabac, I made my way to the main gate. Koabac looked at me with concern as I slipped out.

"Be cautious, alien friend. This is the best time of the day to go, but there will still be patrols out. Try to remain unseen. If you see one of their cannon-wielding vehicles, run as fast as that suit will carry you."

"I'll do everything I can to stay hidden."

"Be safe out there, Guppy." Krell said. 'Don't wind up as leviathan food."

"Thanks. Important safety tip," I said. "Gotta be off if I want to get there before sundown."

"You sure you can find the way?" Krell asked.

"Aside from having guidance from the Eye in the Sky," We still hadn't really briefed the Dohannen military about Dora, but I assumed Krell would soon after I left, "I also have a locator beacon on the other suits to home in on. I'll get there just fine." I started off, and the great gate closed behind me.

I was on my own.

"Mom?" I said. "You there?"

"Always."

"I'm gonna need a vector back to our makeshift base."

"Sending to your HUD, Tanner. This will be a changing path, however. The Ravrath have increased patrols since you made your original journey to the Citadel."

"What's going on? Do you know?"

"I think it comes down to them not finding enough Dohannen to feed to their massive shark god. When in doubt, squeeze the stone harder."

"Oh great." I started moving quickly across the landscape. "I sure hope that means that the Dohannen are getting better at hiding and not what I think you just implied."

Dora didn't reply to that.

"Good God." I said. "This is the most horrifying series of events I can imagine. If we don't get these people out of here..."

"There will be none left," Dora replied. "All fodder for a creature that probably should have gone extinct many millennia ago."

"How could something that voracious even survive? From what I've read, Earth's saber-tooth tigers were such efficient hunters it's believed they literally ate themselves out of house and home. They consumed all the prey in an area and had to move on. They eventually ran out of prey and went extinct. It's a theory, of course, but pretty believable."

"While you were in the Citadel and safe, I was not stationary, Tanner. I know where this leviathan is at all times and I have done extensive scans of it. I've also more closely scanned the ocean floor of this planet. Following your saber-tooth train of thought, I have indeed found the ancient skeletons of more than one of these creatures."

"You mean..?"

"There can be little doubt. The very size of these beings precludes them being preyed upon by anything else other than their own kind."

"Run out of food, resort to cannibalism. Yeesh. Considering the protein needs of something that large, and assuming it can't live on plankton, this is probably the leviathan's last stand."

"I'm not so sure," Dora replied. "There is a lack of larger fish and aqua-mammals on this world, but my analysis indicates this has been a state that has existed for a long time. Almost as if such life was unable to evolve and continue. From my scans, I believe this gigantic creature may be a hibernator. Each time life evolves to be large enough for it to catch, it reemerges."

"That would be a heck of a long time to hibernate."

"This is a new world to us. Nothing can be ruled out. Some of the other leviathan skeletons were ensconced in deep mud and stone. They'd literally been dug out and consumed during what I assume was their hibernation cycle."

"So the one that's left is the king of hell-fish. Don't know how it'll ever reproduce though."

"I'd guess it won't," Dora said. "Maybe, if it can hibernate long enough for sea life to evolve to a size it can use, it will just live forever."

Chapter Twenty

It was a relief to see my own kind, as the gigantic doors to the arena closed behind me. Emily Darkfeather approached me ahead of the others.

"Tanner," she said. "I am so relieved you are back here and safe." She paused, "Well, as safe as we can call ourselves on a hostile-covered planet."

"Believe me," I said as I opened my suit and stepped out, "you're not the only one who's relieved. If I hadn't had Dora guiding me, I'd have had to fight my way here. So many Ravrath out there now."

Emily interrupted me by embracing me in a big hug. She stepped back, a very serious expression on her face. "I don't care if it's against the regulations, I'm realizing that we should take the time to do this sort of thing if we can. Each day might well be the last one we get if things go wrong."

She was very close and looking in my eyes in a way that was very disconcerting. My heart started beating a mile a minute and the room seemed to be getting very warm for some reason. She moved forward, her lips brushed mine and...

A very artificial cough cut into our moment. Commander Torvald was looking discretely in another direction, but obviously wanted my attention. Chief Moreland and Ensign Teo were with him. Emily stepped back, blushing furiously.

"Sir!" I said, trying not to let my voice crack. "Cadet Voss reporting for duty."

"Welcome back, Cadet. Glad to see you," he said, walking up to us. "Nice work at the Citadel. Givall said that the chances you would be able to get his government to help us were not optimal, but it appears you've pulled it off."

"It was not without its hiccups, sir. But with Dora, Krell and Sikall's help, we got things changed to the right direction."

"Excellent. Outstanding work. You'll be pleased to know that as well as trying to save the remaining members of our friend's species we haven't been idle in other areas as well."

"Um… meaning?" I asked.

"We have rigged a shower system and you can use it immediately," Torvald said. "Ensign Teo? Please set the cadet's Mark II to sanitation mode."

"Are you giving me a subtle hint, sir?"

"Subtle? Wasn't going for that, but it's obvious you've spent a lot of time armored up."

I looked over at Emily. "You're pretty brave, you know. I appreciate the hug and moral support."

"Actually, I hugged first," Darkfeather said, "and sniffed second. I'm gonna have to second the shower recommendation." She grinned at me.

"Not a recommendation, actually," Torvald said.

"Understood, sir. Reporting for shower duty."

"Imagine our relief." Chief Moreland chimed in.

"Do you think that you can get us back to this Citadel you went to?"

Doctor Carstairs question was not as straightforward as I would've liked for it to have been. As I sat eating rations, wearing one of Minnie's spare EV under-suits, I had to evaluate a truthful answer to her questions.

"It definitely won't be without risk, Doctor," I replied. "I made it here without incident because Dora kept me vectoring away from Ravrath patrols. I had some close calls though because the Rav tend to zig-zag on their patrol paths. I assume this is an attempt to have a tighter net on any remaining Dohannen but it makes their routes difficult to predict."

"Do you think that Dora will be able to keep them off our necks?"

Emily Darkfeather asked calmly. She was obviously trying to show a calm demeanor for Carstair's benefit.

"I believe so. For all their numbers, from what I've observed they don't have the best visual acuity in the brightest part of the day. You can't help but leave foot prints in a Mark II, but Dora says they've never followed my trail if they crossed it. If we stick to the trees and follow her advice, I'm sure we can get to the Citadel in one piece. And if things go south, we go to plan B."

"And... what exactly," Dr. Carstairs asked, "is plan B?"

"Plan B would come into play if we are spotted. I intend to keep us near the wooded areas as much as possible. If they see us, you and Ensign Darkfeather will slip deeper into the foliage while I charge toward the enemy, speakers blaring a heavy rock song at full volume. I will veer away from them and they will chase after me while you two will slip away."

"Oh my God, Cadet!" Carstairs replied. "That is a suicidal plan. I have no intention of going along with a plan that will surely get you killed. The Dohannen can do without an on-site liaison. Dora has patched all our communications together and we can coordinate via radio transmissions! Or video conferencing."

"The thing is doctor," Emily said. "I need to be there, to see what can be done to enhance the Dohannen military equipment. Our technology has quite a few advances over theirs and I believe if we can combine our tech, the strike parts of our plans could be a lot more successful."

"And, Doctor," I added, "no one but you is an alien culture specialist. Your knowledge may be important in facilitating this whole coordination between our two species."

I could see that Dr. Carstairs was warring between duty and fear. I couldn't really blame her either. The Ravrath were a terrifying enemy engaged in genocide. I was pretty sure our alien status wouldn't protect us in the least. We were all just protein for the leviathan.

◆

I ate, then slept for several hours. After taking care of everything I needed to, I went down to the central command post that Commander Torvald had put together to see where things stood.

"Tanner," the commander said. "You're up! Are you ready to make another trek to the Citadel?"

"Yes sir. I assume the plan hasn't changed and that Dr. Carstairs is on board?"

"Reluctantly. She sees the need for her skills, but, being an intelligent person is very... nervous... about making the trip to aid our allies. Dora reports that Rav patrols are still fairly numerous so you'll be leaving in about an hour, during planetary noon."

"The brightest part of the day. Aye sir."

"I do wish you'd managed to bring one of the Dohannen beam weapons back with you. Darkfeather's going to have to make due with a staff weapon and they're not exactly light. Nor fast firing."

"We'll get by, sir. If we have to fight, we're already in over our heads. Even in my Mark II I'll be going for stealth as job one."

'Good," Torvald said. "Our objective is not to fight a war with the Ravrath, but rather to get the Dohannen to the gate, then back to our time. We want to leave the Rav to their own fate with as little fighting as possible."

"Understood. I'd better go and perform some last minute checks on my suit before we go."

I moved toward the makeshift bay we'd made for the Mark IIs and saw Chief Moreland already going over my unit. He closed a tiny inner hatch and stood up. I heard his knees pop as he did.

"Everything look green, Chief?"

"Yeah, kid. These babies, aside from being heavily armored and shielded, were designed to keep someone alive in vacuum for a couple weeks. Systems are robust. I was just fine-tuning a few things on your rig. I guess you're about ready to head out again?"

"Yeah. As soon as Emily and Doctor Carstairs are set to go."

"This sucks. You shouldn't be the one having to take all these risks."

"I am the most logical choice, Chief. And I know the route."

"Yeah. I know. But you're just a cadet. You should still be at the academy. It isn't fair that you should have to shoulder this risk. It should be me, or one of the officers."

"But Darkfeather is going. She's an officer." I didn't bring up my past triumphs. He knew that if I hadn't been along on the explorer ship's mission, the *Seeker* would've been space dust.

"I know that. She's not much older than you are, Tanner. I don't like that you youngsters are placing your asses on the line like this. It should be old men, like me."

"I understand, Chief. But here we are."

"Yeah. Here we are. You be extra careful out there, kid."

"Roger that."

The chief walked away down one of the hallways, almost at the same moment that Darkfeather and Carstairs emerged from another. Both had makeshift backpacks, and both carried Ravrath staff weapons.

"Cadet Voss, reporting for escort duty, Ensign." I snapped off a smart salute.

Emily Darkfeather gave me the side-eye, not sure if my spit and polish was facetious or not. "Noted, Cadet Voss," she said. "You ready to rumble?"

"I am."

She looked toward the side door we'd slip out of.

"Then let's get this show on the road."

Chapter Twenty-One

In my suit, the only way that I could tell that the day was warm was that my two companions were sweating. The staff weapons they carried were made for the larger-framed Ravrath in powered enviro suits, not for two human females of shorter stature. But neither Emily nor Dr. Carstairs complained and both had death grips on their weapons.

"Tanner," Dora said from somewhere overhead, "Rav patrol ahead. Change your vector twenty degrees to your left."

"Roger that, Mom." With my suit's speakers at their lowest setting, I said to Darkfeather, "Dora says we need to turn twenty, left."

Emily smiled, and pointed to her left ear. I remembered she had her own sub-dermal transceiver and realized the Dora was keeping her in the loop also. We changed direction and moved deeper into the foliage-laden areas.

The Dohannen, in their years becoming land-dwellers, had tamed the mini-continent their civilization had landed on. However, the few years of the Ravrath assault on their civilization were evident in the bioregion's return to a wild state. Cleared fields were full of high grasses and small shrubs. In the city, I'd noticed that any crack in the infrastructure had started to sprout weeds and grasses, sure signs that a civilization was on the decline.

Watching my HUD I saw our vector and that of the Rav patrol eventually begin to separate. A few minutes later, I notice another red dot indicating a new patrol on the upper left corner of my HUD's map. If they stayed on that course, we'd need to correct again.

"Tanner? You seeing what I'm seeing?" Darkfeather asked, looking down at her padd.

"Yeah. I sure don't like being between two sets of Rav."

"I think if we turn a little bit to the right here, we can avoid both patrols. Plus, it's heavily forested there. What do you think?"

I was about to consult Dora when I hesitated. Did I really want to be seen as a guy who couldn't make a decision for myself? Especially when Emily knew the whole story of Dora being my AI mom?

Yeah. My pride shuddered at the thought.

"I think that's a good idea. It's mid-way between our original vector and Dora's last change. Let's do it." I hoped that both enemy patrols would keep heading in their current lines of movement. If they did, they'd surely miss us, especially in the cover the forest provided.

Moving quietly in an engineering suit isn't the easiest thing in the world, and I winced as my exterior microphones picked up every branch I stepped on. I was doing my best to place my feet carefully, but there's only so much you can do in eleven hundred pounds of armor. I careful looked around and noted that even through my visor, I could make out my own tracks behind us. I prayed that the Ravrath's ocean origins made the concept of tracking foreign to them.

"Southern patrol has changed direction," Dora said. "Vector left ten degrees." There was no argument by either Darkfeather or myself, but both of us knew that course would put us closer to the northern patrol. It felt like being in a net that was tightening.

"Oh, I don't like this," Darkfeather said.

She wasn't alone. I hadn't been sweating in my armor before, but I was now. Heat had nothing to do with it. My sweating turned into a racing heart as the southern patrol turned in our general direction.

"Oh crap." Darkfeather said.

"What is it?" Dr. Carstairs said, anxiety writ large across her face.

"Mom?" I said. "Our vector is narrowing quickly. Got any ideas? From what I see, there's a good chance we're going to cross paths with these bastards."

"Tanner… son. Unless both patrols turn in the next five minutes, the chances that you will be seen are almost ninety percent. My only suggestion is that Ensign Darkfeather and Dr. Carstairs crawl on their bellies through the thickets and you continue forward without them. And prepare for Plan B."

"Understood."

"Tanner, you don't need to…" Darkfeather said.

"Yes, Emily. Yes I do. You two hunker down. I got this."

I could see she wanted to argue, but she could see how deep we were in it. She dropped down low and motioned for Carstairs to join her. They both side-crawled back under the brush.

"Alright, I'll see you both later. Count on it." I moved ahead through the forest and saw an opening where both sets of Ravrath would be able to see me. My padd was at my hip, and through my suit's HUD I wirelessly chose a song from the playlist my dad had gifted me, but didn't activate it. I wanted it to look like I had been seen accidentally through carelessness. The rock and roll was for when things got hairy.

As I reached the opening, I stepped out into full view, looking as clueless as I could. I wanted the Rav to believe I'd made a stupid error instead of believing I was showing myself on purpose to distract them. The response was almost instantaneous.

"Tanner," Dora said. "Both groups are accelerating toward your position. Whatever you're going to do, this is a good time to do it."

"Copy." I turned toward the southern group, the group which was toward the ocean and started running. The Mark II's have a top speed of almost thirty miles per hour, and it's limitation is the fitness and stamina of the person inside it. Since my academy courses mentor on the *Seeker* was Chief Kurakin, head of security, I did daily PT with her people. That meant training in the 1.5 gravity section of the athletics room.

In other words, stamina wasn't going to be a problem. I'd lead these jack-holes on a merry chase and hopefully they'd never have a clue that I hadn't been alone.

"Tanner, you're running directly at the southernmost force," Dora said.

"All part of the plan, Mom. I can see the enemy positions on my HUD map." The small map in the lower right side of my view plate had enough red dots on it you might think it had acquired a case of the measles.

The leading soldiers of the force I was heading for began firing their staff weapons at me. The charged water projectiles were slower than a bullet, and I began weaving to try to avoid them. One pinged off the shielding on my right arm, but the force of it still almost spun me around. Time to change vectors.

I turned thirty degrees to my right and again started running as fast as the suit would go. The power-assist to my muscles propelled my armored form to its maximum. A tiny side screen on the left edge of my HUD showed me the rearview and I could see great clumps of sod flying up behind me. Beyond, I could see the Ravs on their odd little scooters.

"Dora," I said as I sprinted, "is there any way to subvert the Ravrath scoots? It... strikes me that if we could find a way... to shut down their vehicles, we'd have a distinct advantage."

"The conveyances that they're pursuing you with are very basic, and not networked in any way. I will continue to analyze this idea, but at this point I'd need a heavy-duty EMP to scramble these machines and that would indiscriminately target friend and foe."

"Wish we had an EMP beam weapon, mom."

"Intriguing idea. But for now, concentrate on the current situation."

She was right. A water-blast hit me square in the back, flashing the suit's shielding into visibility. I stumbled, but was able to stay upright and began to run a varied evasive path. It slowed me down, but the Rav were already having trouble hitting me with all of us on the move. I just wanted to make their aim even worse.

A proximity alarm in my suit pinged and swiveling my helmet to the left I saw one industrious overachiever had managed to catch me and was lining up for a 'can't miss' shot. I decided that wasn't in my best interest, and changed vector into him. The resultant crash barely bumped me but my opponent went end over end, with his scoot landing on him as he plowed the dirt.

"Tanner," Dora said, "I am reading a large group of people on roughly the same vector that you are on. It's a large group of Dohannen... and it appears they are being herded by the Rav. They're almost to the ocean."

"Well, of course," I muttered. "As if I don't have enough problems." I changed direction slightly and headed toward the ocean.

I dashed through a small outcropping of forest and was pleased to see my pursuers hard-pressed to get their small vehicles through the vegetation. Something to file away for later usage. As I broke through, the ocean spread out before me. We'd been closer than I thought.

Ahead, I could see a large group of people being herded by Rav. The enemy were on their standard scoots, but one larger vehicle rolled along behind armed with what looked like a large firehose. A few moments later I saw that was exactly what it was.

The ocean was a good ways below the plateau we were on, and I was mortified to see the firehose employed to shove the Dohannen over the edge.

"Mom! Are the sending them over a cliff?"

"Negative, though it is approximately a seventy-five degree incline, very muddy. There is an inlet there where the Dohannen are coming to rest."

"Any sign of the leviathan?"

"Yes. It is approaching rapidly from the southwest. The Ravrath must have some underwater signal they're using to summon it."

"Well, let's add our input to their plan."

"Be careful Tanner! If you are are being overwhelmed, I expect you to break off and run. Am I clear, young man?"

"Yes, ma'am." I looked at the input icon on my HUD and activated external speakers. "Activate playlist item Led Zeppelin, Rock and Roll. Maximum volume."

The Ravs hadn't noticed I was coming at them, being very centered on herding their charges into the ocean and their doom. My speakers, blaring out 20th century music at a deafening decibel level definitely got their attention. It also threw them into a panic and by the time I reached the larger vehicle no one had gotten a shot off at me.

The Mark II suit was once demonstrated back on Earth by lifting the front end of a military tank over the demonstrator's head. The fire hose vehicle was by no means anywhere near that heavy. When I grabbed the side of it with both gauntlets and heaved, instead of flopping over on its side, it flipped in mid-air, landed on its treads again then bounced and flopped over on its side. The Rav who'd been manning the water cannon damn near went into orbit, landing somewhere in the ocean.

Several of the herded Dohannen took this opportunity to run for their lives. Though they'd been ocean dwellers previously, they didn't have the large finned feet of the Rav and their captors had to resort to their scoots to chase them. I did my best to keep the aquatic bastards off their game by knocking them off their scooters when I could catch them.

"Tanner, you are being surrounded," Dora said. "Break off and flee the scene."

Several Dohannen were almost to the tree line behind us, and I knew if they could get into the thickets there, they might have a fighting chance of evading their captors. I kept slugging when I probably should have been running.

"Tanner The Rav are bringing up another vehicle. Get out of there!"

I knocked another enemy soldier off his scoot, and turned to face this new menace. The craft's water cannon was aimed directly at me but when the spray hit, it didn't even rock me slightly. Then I noticed it wasn't really aimed at me. It was knocking the remaining Dohannen off their feet and down the slope to the inlet. I started toward the vehicle to re-enact my earlier attack on this new enemy. The Rav saw me coming, and turned the cannon on me. It slowed me slightly, but I wasn't impressed.

"That all you got?" I yelled, superseding my blaring music. The volume alone made the Ravs wince, but I quickly found out that no, that level of cannon force was NOT all they had to give. They had a lot more to send my way.

The power of the water cannon doubled, and I definitely felt it. Then it tripled. And quadrupled. Now it wasn't a matter of me being slowed down, it was a matter of staying upright. And I was definitely losing ground.

The foot soldiers began blasting me with their staff weapons in a coordinated assault, and I was losing ground very quickly. The aft camera in the corner of the HUD showed that I was very near the lip of the slope to the inlet.

"Tanner! They're pushing you over the edge!" Dora said, desperation in her voice. "Get out of there!"

"I'm trying! I can't get traction!" Just then, I felt the land slip out from under me and I began sliding down the slope. "Look out below!"

The Dohannen in the inlet scrambled to get out of the way of my massive bulk, screaming as they fled. I came to a halt in a few feet of water. The people there crowded around me, hoping I had some sort of magic techno-trick to save them.

"Help us! Get us out of here!" A hysterical woman began screaming at me. I didn't blame her for that, I felt like screaming myself. I blinked at my HUD until my external speakers went to normal.

"Is there any way you all can climb out?" I asked.

"Not much chance of that," A man with the remains of a security suit said, gesturing at the rim of the drop. Rav now surrounded the edge and were aiming down at the crowd. Anyone who tried to climb out would be knocked on their ass.

"Tanner, can you use your magna thrusters to climb that hill?" Dora asked.

"I can't leave these people to die, mom!"

"You might, however, if you can get up there, be able to knock the Rav out of the way, and these people might be able to either climb out or swim along the seashore until they can get out without Rav interference."

"All right, I'll give it a shot," I said. Turning to the security officer, I told him my plan.

"I'll take any chance we can get," he said. "Go get them."

I turned and started up the hill. The thrusters on my suit were intended for weightless vacuum, but they were able to get a little additional forward momentum for me as I tried to go up the slippery slope. I was making headway, almost reaching the halfway point when the first staff projectile hit me, flaring my shields. Then another, another, then multiple hits. Between the impacts and the mud, I was sliding back. An alert on my HUD flashed, warning me that my ion-based thrusters were almost out of charge, then they cut out. Without the extra boost I slid back down the hill.

Setting the thrusters to recharge from my armor's fusion generator, I looked around at the Dohannen in the pit with me. All were looking out to sea.

Looking where they were looking, I saw a fin crest the waves. I thought it was big when it appeared, but it just kept growing and when it swam in front of a small forested island, I had a reference for scale. The fin alone must've been six stories in height. The beast it was attached to was probably the size of an old-world aircraft carrier.

"Holy heck," I whispered. "Mom? You seeing this?"

"Yes," she replied softly, "Tanner, it's starting toward the beach. Can't you get out of there?"

"No such luck. Can't get up that hill with all the Rav knocking me back down."

"I've observed it's modus operandi earlier. It will force a tsunami into the inlet almost filling it, and the rip-tide that it creates will carry everyone out into the ocean and it's maw. You will need to grab a sturdy rock and use your suit to hold on for dear life. Hopefully you will be able to withstand the tidal forces."

"This is beyond the point where you can save anyone but yourself.

Perhaps a few of them will be able to hang onto your armor but most of them are doomed. You cannot change that now."

"No, that's not…" I hesitated as my external mics picked up cries of terror from the Dohannen surrounding me. Looking back toward the ocean, I saw why. A huge wave was rushing in toward us, the kind of wave surfers get crushed in. It towered over our small group and I could see the sky through it. I could also see a large terrifying shape though the water behind it, following the tsunami in.

"Listen everyone!" The security officer yelled, getting everyone's attention. "The wave's going to hit us then pull us outward toward the beast. Try your hardest to swim to the sides and along the shore! Move! Make for the edges now! Swim like Frang!"

His short speech galvanized everyone. The panicked crowd all surged toward the edges, and the Ravs up top began firing into them. People were knocked down and trampled, but no one was giving up on getting to the sides of the inlet.

Then it was too late. The wave was less than fifty yards away and I knew that it was time to listen to Dora. I looked around, saw a boulder that looked to be part of the bedrock and kneeled getting a death grip on the stone. Someone had come over to stand beside me and as I looked over, I was shocked to realize that I knew this person. It was Dekell, the woman who'd been exiled. I guessed that Kivar was somewhere nearby.

"Please," she said. "I see what you're trying to do. Can I please hold on to you? This… I can't…" Large limpid tears filled her eyes.

"Crawl under me," I said. "Hang onto the suit. Maybe there's a long-shot chance that we can survive the force of the wave."

She did, and in the few seconds it took her to do so, the wave hit us. It only took that to make me realize that all our hopes of escaping were probably forlorn. The sheer impact almost tore me loose from my perch and all the people around and on the edge were slammed toward the land end of the inlet in a wash of flying Dohannen.

For a moment, there was no force one way or another then, the surge began inexorably to flow back toward the ocean. We weren't slammed as we were with the wave going in, but now tons of water were trying return to their main body and everything in the inlet was going with it. Dohannen were flashing past me, trying to get a grip on anything they could to avoid being pulled out, including my armor. As more an more flashed past, several were able to gain hand holds on my armor, and the drag on the suit increased.

Suddenly, the edge of stone I was gripping broke loose and we all went with the wave. I tumbled slower than the rest due to the weight of my armor, and I could see that the situation was hopeless regarding saving anyone else. At this point, it was every sentient for themselves.

I checked my HUD and saw my thrusters had recharged. I aimed for the edge of the inlet and fired them off. I'd definitely get a lot more efficiency in water than I would in dry land. I had a thrust-assisted crawl toward the edge when I realized I wasn't alone. Dekell was clinging to the front of my suit, eyes screwed tightly shut.

Maybe I can save one other person.

I put my left arm around her and redoubled my efforts to get to the edge. The ground in the inlet had been sand and rock, but as we were pulled farther out, it changed to slimy mud and I couldn't get traction. The rip tide swept my feet out from under me and we were spinning end-over-end toward a huge dark shape in the water.

I corrected my spin with my thrusters then aimed for the edge of the death zone. There's no real swimming with a Mark II, so it was all up to the thrusters, as I watched the available thruster power level drop at an alarming rate. Out of the corner of my faceplate, I saw the forward edge of a huge appendage. We were approaching it quickly, and turning my head slightly I got my first good look at the monster. It was a nightmare. It's huge maw was surrounded by petal-like flaps that were covered with teeth and spikes. I could see swimming Dohannen being skewered on them.

Dekell and I were almost to the outer edge of the creature's mouth circumference. Just a bit more, and we'd be out of immediate danger. I could see a few Dohannen had made it past that point and were frantically swimming toward the shore. Just a bit more and we'd be there. The outer edge of the closest flap rushed toward us and I could see it was going to be close.

No. It wasn't. We were just a tiny bit too far in and my thrusters were almost exhausted from pushing through the water. I wasn't going to clear the edge. I pulled Dekell loose, and as we came to the edge, I heaved her clear, while I wound up going the wrong way.

For a moment, I could see the outline of her form, then I began tumbling into the black maw from the abyss.

Chapter Twenty-Two

Blackness. I fell into the the huge mouth and what little light was coming through the water was snuffed out. I switched on my light bands to see what I was up against.

I wish I hadn't. Oh dear God, I wished I hadn't.

My lights illuminated a scene that Dante Alighieri would have recognized. Not an inferno, but definitely a vista from Hell. A being that had lived as long as the leviathan would, of course, had a very efficient system for processing food. It didn't care how horrific that was to its prey.

The entire throat was lined with stationary spikes, each around six feet or more in length. These alternated with huge flat elongated teeth with deep-set serrations running up each side which waved back and forth through muscular contraction. When prey came down the tube, they worked in tandem. In my suit's lights, I saw the Dohannen who'd been in the inlet with me impaled on the spikes, then the teeth would wave and slash, taking limbs, heads or cutting the people in half. There was purplish blood everywhere, splattering across my faceplate, only to washed away by tons of seawater.

The skewers bounced off my body but the serrated teeth ground against the armor. With my shields flaring, I grabbed one of the great teeth to stop myself from sliding down the monster's gullet, my gauntlets flaring as the serrations tried to cut through them.

I wanted to do something, anything to help these people avoid their fate, but the problem was just too big. By the time I stabilized my self against one wall of the leviathan's mouth, there was nobody left alive, just a slurry of what had once been living breathing sentients and was now just a river of blood and body parts.

As I clung for dear life, the beast must've been cognizant of my presence in the same way a human would be aware of a piece of hamburger caught in their teeth. It began to convulse the tissues and teeth around me, trying to shake me loose.

"Tanner … can…read…" Dora's static-laden voice came over my transceiver.

"I hear you, Mom. I'm still alive. I'm the only one alive."

"You're near... wall. You must... get... before it dives."

She was right. My safety was only temporary. If the leviathan dived, chances are that the pressure from the ocean depths might even overwhelm a Mark II. But I just couldn't seem to think straight.

"Mom, I... I don't know what to do!"

"Listen... me. Plasma..." her voice trailed off. The beast must be diving. But I knew what she meant. My danger sense was telling me right where I needed to strike. That I hadn't listened to it immediately, spoke volumes about how rattled I was.

I checked my indicators. Thrusters were back up to twenty percent but my right arm plasma cutter, on a different battery, was at one hundred. I turned to my left to where my talent told me to attack. I ignited the cutter, which was used for cutting heavy steel plating, and began to burrow out of the leviathan.

I didn't want to identify with the monster in any way, but I assumed my cutting a path sideways out of its mouth would feel a lot like a human biting their cheek. The more I hurt this huge being, the more my mind sharpened back up. The immediate effects of the trauma of watching so many die so horribly was shoved to the back of my psyche.

There wasn't a lot of gore from the beast. The plasma cutter cauterized as it cut, but the further I burrowed into what was essentially its cheek, the more the leviathan began to struggle. I was slammed back and forth in the cavity I had cut. As I tunneled closer to the outer skin, Dora was able to transmit to me with less and less interference.

"Tanner, my scanning indicates that you are almost to the exterior. What is your thruster status?"

"At about fifty-percent charge. How deep are we?"

"Two hundred twenty four feet. Your Mark II should be able to handle that level of external pressure. The leviathan is resting on the bottom on a shelf next to an abyss, and you need to make haste before it decides to go deeper."

"Is it doing anything besides sitting there?"

It's stirring up great turbidity in the water, though that seems to be a byproduct of the pain it is experiencing, not a conscious activity. It really doesn't like what you're doing."

"Good," I said, more than happy to cause the creature as much pain as possible. "What's the terrain toward shore like?"

"Fortunately, it is a sloping drop. We are also fortunate that the creature did not make for deeper water. The depth you are at shouldn't compromise your suit, but much deeper and you'd have been in danger of implosion."

"Distance to shore?"

"Roughly 1.12 miles."

"Chances that this creature won't try to interfere?"

"Too many variables and not enough data. My opinion is that you will need to use the turbidity and stealth to make it to shore."

Just then, a burst of water hit me in the chest plate. I'd burned through to the ocean and with a couple more cuts, I was out. I tumbled from the beast and sparingly used my thrusters to right myself so I'd land feet first on the bottom.

I wound up facing back toward the leviathan as I dropped, and I saw it was moving again. Seconds later, an eye the size of a swimming pool appeared and looked at me. Immediately I felt an intense pressure on my mind. A malevolent hatred looked down upon me and I knew I wasn't going to get to shore easily.

The great religions of Earth tell us to meet hate with love, but in this case, I returned, through that telepathic link, a hate equal in measure to what I was receiving. No great concepts, no attempt at first contact, just a mutual desire to see the other wiped from existence. We both knew how the other felt.

It disappeared into the murk and darkness but from what we'd shared, I knew it would be back.

"Mom," I said, turning off all my suit's external lighting, "I need a vector toward shore. It's gonna come for me, and my only chance to make it will be for me to be hard to find."

"On your HUD now, Tanner. The beast is about three miles out to sea, but it appears to be turning back toward your position."

"Let me know when it might be in visual range and I'll freeze. Hopefully it can't see into the infra-red spectrum."

"Set your suit to its coldest setting, just in case," Dora replied. "It has just sped up. Is the floor muddy or sandy there?"

"Muddy. Kinda thick, slowing me down."

"Drop down and cover yourself as much as you can. Unless the creature can see your heat signature through the armor, the mud might make such a large creature miss a small person such as yourself."

"Well, now I know what you think of me," I said, bellyflopping into the mud and brushing it over and behind me.

"Not the time for sass, young man. It's coming. Be completely still."

I lay there, not daring to move a muscle. My head was turned slightly so I could see out of the side of my faceplate as I waited. Moments later, a huge bulk loomed out of the darkness and filled my limited field of vision. It took a full two minutes to pass over me and then it was gone.

"It doesn't know exactly where you are, and it has gone out to sea, presumably for another pass. Move Tanner!"

I moved. I pushed off from the mud and began moving with thruster assist for the shore. I knew the monster was fast in the water, but it also had a huge bulk it needed to navigate back to my position. The last pass indicated it didn't know exactly where we'd parted.

"Tanner. It reacted as soon as you used your thrusters! Cut them now."

I cut the thrusters. Now I was trudging toward shore at the pace of a slow walk. At this speed, I'd reach the land in an hour, at least.

"It's coming around again," Dora said. "I think somehow it could echo-locate you through the thrusters. It seems to be heading directly for you. Into the mud!"

Into the sludge I went. With each pass the creature made, its flukes stirred the bottom, which raised the mud. I hope it wouldn't be smart enough to let everything settle before coming after me. I needn't have worried on that account, the leviathan had an entirely different strategy in mind.

As I lay on my side, covered in a layer of mud and silt, the sky above the waves was blotted out again. The beast passed over and I thought I was clear, right until someone set off a huge bomb a short ways away from me. The half ton of Mark II armor lifted ten feet off the bottom before settling back down into the now swirling mud and sand.

"Mom! What the hell just happened?"

"The creature slammed its tail into the ocean floor. It is trying to pulverize you, even if it can't find you."

"I can literally feel the hate emanating from its mind," I told her. "I think it must be at least partially telepathic."

"Then listen to me carefully, Tanner. You must empty your mind of thought. If its sensing anything from you, then it knows you're alive. It seems to be very single minded in its thirst for revenge. Remember your meditation training from your martial arts classes. Clear your mind."

I did my best. Suddenly being told to go into an empty-mind state may sound good, but it's harder than you might think. Especially if other matters have kept you from your meditation practice. I had the tools, I just needed to make them work, lying face down in mud under the waters of an alien ocean with a gigantic creature trying to find and crush me. No worries.

I imagined sinking down into my own psyche, like sinking into a cool mountain lake.

THOOM!

I again raised off the ocean floor and settled back into the mud.

Thoom!

That one seemed farther off. I noted this and went back into a blank mind state as I sank back into the mud. The tail strikes went on for another fifteen minutes, growing farther away with each strike. My suit was set for cool temperatures and I began shivering, but I didn't move even a little to try and warm up. Possible hypothermia was outweighed by possible flattening.

Then, silence. My external mic picking out only the sounds of the currents and various aquatic creatures too small to be threatened by the monster. I didn't move. My step dad had sent Valiel and I to numerous survival and hunting classes in our teens and one thing successful prey learned was not to move too soon. The old experienced bucks could hide ten feet from you, and you'd have no idea they were there. That's what I was going for.

"Tanner. It has gone out to sea and submerged very deeply. I believe it's satisfied that you are dead. Start moving toward the shore, no thrusters to begin with. Just make progress inland."

I stood and began the long trudge to get out of the ocean. It was slow going, and I was cold, but I was also highly motivated. My main concern was that the monster was just testing to see if I'd grow careless. The mud was dissipating, sinking back to the bottom and the water was growing clearer.

Eventually I came to a reef system. The water was growing more shallow and I had to chart a winding path between large formations of alien coral.

"Any sign of it, Mom? I'd really like to stop walking and start gliding with my thrusters."

"It is out to sea about twenty miles and below the surface at a depth of eight hundred feet, but it is not moving out of this general area. And, it is being very still for an aquatic creature. Tanner, I believe it is listening for you. I think using your thrusters would be a very bad idea."

"That sounds like it's more intelligent than we might have thought. I kinda began to suspect that when we were touching telepathically. The hatred it sent me seemed to be beyond just animal anger."

"All the more reason to be very cautious, Tanner."

"All right, more trudging," I said. "I'm gonna bring up my suit's temperature, though. I'm about shivered out and I'm worried about actual hypothermia."

"I strongly doubt it will be able to sense your heat signature at this distance."

She was right. After walking over and climbing across several series of reefs, I was exhausted, even in my suit. So when my helmet actually rose above the water it surprised me. I was about a hundred yards from the beach. It was the dead of night, and borealis effect in the sky was amazing after hours in the murk.

'Tanner, there are four Dohannen waiting on the shore for you. They are the survivors of the massacre."

"How'd you get them here to meet me?"

"One of them had a comm device I was able to hack into. I directed them here so that they could accompany you back to the events center."

The darkness was by no means absolute with all the light flashing across the sky. I flipped over to my HUD's night-vision mode and the people waiting on shore seemed to magically appear. There were two Dohannen that I didn't know, the security officer, who must've been the one with the comm unit, and Dekell. I had managed to save one person, even though her own people had banished her to certain death.

As far as I was concerned, she had survived her sentence, and I had commuted it. Anyone who cared to argue could take it up with a very tired, possibly cranky fellow in a very heavy armored suit.

Chapter Twenty-Three

"And this is why I love the Laldoralins," Chief Moreland said. "The tech they've given us, aside from being top notch, is tougher than nails."

I sat on a bench watching him tinker with my suit, which was hanging from a pair of chains. For all his words, to me, the Mark II looked like it had survived a world war.

"It may look bad," he continued, "but I can fix it with spares from Minnie's locker. Put that against any tech we had before Earth joined the Hegemony and the old stuff would've been shredded by that big fish. Or flattened."

"Yeah."

Shredded. Like all those people.

"Look, Cadet, I know you went through hell out there. And when we get back to the *Seeker,* and we are getting back, I'm gonna recommend to the captain that you are going to see counselor Mendez on a very regular basis."

Oh joy. Something to look forward to.

"But right now," he continued, "we're still in the deep and brown. I'd love nothing better than to put you on 'administrative duties' but I need you to come back from wherever your head is dragging you and be present and ready for action."

"The young warrior is very traumatized," a soft female voice said from the door. Dekell walked into our makeshift repair bay. "He's not the only one. I have never been so terrified in my entire life. Not even when the others banished Kivar and I. And what Tanner went through is a thousand times worse."

"I know that, lady," the chief replied. "But it doesn't change our situation. There's a time to grieve and process things, but we are near the edge of a major confrontation with a numerically far superior force. We're only going to survive and get out of here if we bring our 'A' game."

"I do not know what you mean by this 'A' game, Chief Moreland."

"What he means is," I interrupted, "I need to get my head right. To push my emotions aside and do my duty. And he's correct, but every time I try to sleep, all I can see is those people being torn apart and blood everywhere." I rubbed my eyes as if that would clear the visions away.

"I may have a solution for that in the first aid kit on the miner," Chief Moreland said. "Minnie was meant to be out for weeks at a time, and its two-man crew has to be able to get sleep while the mining process progressed. Consequently, there's a theta state tuner on board. It's a temporary fix, it won't help with your memories, but you'll be able to sleep without dreaming. I'll go talk to the Commander about it."

"Yes, Chief."

"In the meantime, go into Minnie and use the small printer there to replace this LR-85 in the right knee joint. This is the cause of the limp you started experiencing on your way back from the ocean."

"Understood. Will do."

I walked to the back of the huge area and trudged up Minnie the Miner's rear access ramp. The chief was right. I needed to get it together, but telling yourself that wasn't the same as actually being able to do it. The more I wanted to clamp down on this, the worse it seemed to get.

I double-checked the part number on the component, and keyed it into the printer. Then, I set the printer to de-molecularize the existing bad part. Once the LR-85 node had been reduced to its component elements, the printer began to reform the part into a factory-fresh version. A tone, followed by a red flashing light, noted that I needed to supplement the process with a small amount of magnesium so I walked over to the supply racks and found a small bottle of the powdered stuff. Attaching it to the element intake coupling, the printer was able to extract exactly the amount it needed.

On board the *Seeker*, this latter part of the process would be unnecessary. The large printers back on the ship had immediate access to all the elements they required so there was no need for operator assistance. The printer on Minnie was small, intended for emergency part repair and without all the frills of its larger cousins. Nonetheless, ten minutes later I had a fresh LR-85 node in my hands ready to replace in my Mark II. I was almost through the process when someone walked up behind me.

"Cadet Voss," Commander Torvald said, as I stood to attention.

"Yes, sir. Just getting my Mark II back in shape for the coming action, sir."

"At ease, Tanner. The chief tells me you are unable to sleep for any amount of time. A bit of PTSD I'm thinking."

"Maybe, Commander."

"I can't imagine… from your report.. I… Oh dammit, Cadet. Your made a side trip through hell and if I could, I'd bench you for a psych eval, but as you know, we're up against it."

"I can carry my weight, sir."

"I don't doubt it, Cadet," Torvald said, "but you can't do it if you're so sleep deprived that you can't function. So, I'm going to have you follow me to your rack and the chief can finish repairs on your suit."

We walked into a communal area that had several large closets. Torvald, Carstairs and Darkfeather were bunking in the three bunks in the miner. Ping, the chief and I had improvised beds out of padded stadium seats, stacking them and welding them together. They were actually pretty comfortable if you were a reasonably still sleeper.

I walked over to mine, and Torvald brought out a mechanical headband and slid it onto my forehead.

"Lay down, Taner. You ever used one of these?" He asked.

"No sir, can't say that I have. I'm not sure that any of this will do any good. My mind just won't shut down and…" Torvald pushed a button on the band and I never finished the sentence.

◆

"Rise and shine, Cadet," a voice said. "We've got a busy day ahead."

My head felt like it was full of cotton, but I sat up and pushed my makeshift blanket off.

"Here, drink this." The person behind the voice handed me a cup of some sort and an aromatic scent rose from the surface through the steam.

"What?" I replied with scintillating razor-sharp brilliance.

"Kobec," the voice said. "Tea," the translator intoned.

I drank the hot liquid, only mildly burning myself and the cobwebs began to clear away. I looked up, and the voice turned out to be Ensign Teo watching me with a slight smirk.

"Did we have us a nice nap, Cadet?" She said as if talking to a two-year-old.

"Yes, Auntie Ping. We sure did. What's happening?"

"It's 'storm the power plant' day, Tanner. And you, the chief and I are going to get to smack some Rav in the process. You in?"

The thought of giving payback to the Ravrath woke in me an anger, a hatred that surprised me. "Oh yes. I am in."

The expression on my face made the ensign pause. I'm sure it wasn't a nice one. I'm sure it wasn't nice at all.

"You okay there, Tanner?" She asked, and I could see the worry on her face.

"Can't actually say that I am, Ma'am. But I'm functional and that's what the commander needs, isn't it?"

"I'm afraid so. The commander will be briefing us in twenty minutes in the common area. See you there, okay?"

"Aye aye." I replied. "Do you know if my armor is green-lighted?"

"The chief put it through some hard paces this morning when he and I took a little patrol around town. He says it'll hold up, though he wants all of our Mark IIs to get a full refurbish when we get back to *Seeker.*"

"Good. I put mine through the wood chipper. Damn those things are tough."

"Good ol' Lallie tech. See you in twenty," she said as she went out the door.

◆

"So, basically, we're the diversionary force."

Commander Torvald stepped back from the hologram being projected from Minnie's unit through a jury-rigged emitter sitting on one of the miner's treads. "We'll be moving against the Ravrath at this point to the south to draw them out and weaken their defense of the power plant. Once they start chasing us, we fall back into retreat mode and hopefully they'll continue after us so the Dohannen military can hit them from the rear."

"Seems like kind of a tall order for three engineering suits and a handful of civilians to pull off, sir," Ensign Teo said, moving up to see the details of the holographic terrain better. "Especially with our lack of any weapons except the Rav's own staff blasters."

"I believe Dunar has some happy news on that front," Chief Moreland said. "He's been joining me on my patrol around town, and when he found out what we had to fight with, he showed me where the town armory was. I'd have never found it on my own."

Dunar, the security officer who'd survived the leviathan, stepped forward carrying an oval-shaped hardshell case. He opened it, and pulled out one of the beam weapons similar to those I'd seen at the citadel. "These lasers are far better long-range weapons than anything we've seen from the Rav, better weapons all around. We also have one larger version intended for emplacements, that throws a large amount of energy downstream. Enough to take out any of their hovercraft, if we can get our shot off first."

"Is it transportable?" Ping asked.

"Having seen what your armored suits can do, I'm quite sure that it can be carried by one person and the mount and power source can be carried by another. Also, if we have to abandon it, which seems likely when we retreat, it can be set to explode behind us."

"Wow," Ping said. "If your weapons are better, how'd the Rav get the upper hand like this?"

"They outnumbered us ten to one. Also, our politicians were slow to understand how dire the situation was, thinking it was just another one of the Rav's regular 'poking us to see if we bleed' cycles. By the time the higher-ups acknowledged that it was war, we were already half defeated."

"Politicians." Moreland said with acid in his tone,

"Politicians," Dunar agreed. "But every Dohannen alive now knows what the stakes are and we are ready to fight."

"Outstanding," Torvald said. "But I want to stress, none of you civilians need to help on this. You've had your lives in peril so much already, I can't in good conscience ask you to assist us with this."

Dekell, who'd been watching and listening from the back of the group, stepped forward. I still wasn't a hundred percent at reading Dohannen facial expressions, but her body language seemed very determined.

"Commander Torvald," she said, "All of us here know what's happening in our world. We're in a situation where we fight or be exterminated. Every one of us here had that proven to us in a very emphatic way when the Rav tried to feed us to their god. We all know that there is no longer such a thing as a Dohannen civilian. We're in." The other few survivors gave rumbles of agreement.

"Then," Torvald replied, "welcome to the team." He looked toward the two children that had come in with Givall and Lallal. "Anyone who can't run fast should be ready to stay behind and provide logistical support. When the tides turn, we'll need to leave the field of battle in a hurry, and hope your military forces can take the plant during our distraction. Lalall and Givall, I want you to stay here. We can't afford to lose you."

"There are a few other considerations also, once we've captured the plant," Emily Darkfeather said through the link with the Citadel. She and Carstairs had made it there after I drew all the Rav away from them. "We'll also need to keep the power lines from being cut by the Rav again, and we'll need to garrison the portal gate. Captain Koabac's intelligence people believe that our enemy doesn't really grasp what it is, but just know that we consider it important. Since the Dohannen retreated to the citadel the Rav have practically ignored it."

"Then it may just be a matter of picking off any patrols that come into that area before they can give us away," Dunar said.

"I'll gladly volunteer for that," I said. "I can assure you, if I can get within arms reach, any Rav in the area won't be worrying about reporting back in. Ever." As I said it, I heard the angry growl in my own voice. It surprised me a little. I wasn't the only one. Everyone was looking at me with concerned expressions.

"Cadet," Torvald said, giving me a searching, stern look, "I know you've been through a horrible experience at the hands of our enemy. But let me make this perfectly clear to you. This is a precision operation. There is no place for looking to get payback here. If I see you going out to get some cowboy vengeance I swear to you I will pull you from duty and climb into that Mark II myself. I may not have much time in one compared to you using one, but even a noob will be better than someone whose emotions compromise the mission. Am I clear?"

"Yes sir."

"I didn't hear that, cadet!"

"Sir! Yes sir!" I shouted. I felt my face turning red.

"Yes sir what, Voss?"

"I will be calm and precise, sir! No vengeance seeking."

"Good. Remember that promise. Now, we've all been over the plan enough times I think we're done here. We leave at first light to catch our enemy in brightest daylight. Everyone needs to be rested. Check your gear, rest, get fed and be ready in the morning."

Everyone filed out and as I went to get a little fresh air on the roof, my padd pinged from my belt. Dora was relaying a video call from Emily Darkfeather.

"Hello, Ensign," I said. "Are you calling to chew my butt too?"

Her worried face looked out at me from my device. "I'm not calling ensign to cadet, Tanner. I'm calling as your friend."

I looked at her worried face through the screen. "I appreciate that, I really do, but please don't go all sympathetic on me. I can take a dressing down by the commander. It forces me to pick myself up and dust myself off. But I think we all know I'm not in a great head space here."

"I figured."

"Thing is, fussing over me and being motherly is just going to make things worse. I need to be hard right now, I can't be soft and hold it together. Can you understand that?"

"Yes. Yes I can, Tanner."

"I can get help once we're home and I admit to you that I have a serious hate in my heart for the Ravrath. If you'd only seen what they did to those people… but… I need to keep my shit together for the coming action."

"I have faith in you to do your job, Tanner Voss. You won't let the team down."

"Thanks Emily. The commander didn't tell us how your mission is going. Any luck enhancing the weaponry of our allies?"

"A few modulation improvements that will increase the power on all their beam weapons and if we had more time I could probably do even more. My best effort though is a new linked gun system using their battle rifles rigged in tandem. Racking four battle rifles together, we've a got an infinite multi-firing weapon that can be mounted on any vehicle."

"Will the Dohannen be driving them?"

"Dora can access them remotely and free up the soldiers for other tasks," she said. "The linked rifles will have a very high rate of fire. Their weapons were designed for single-shot discharge, but by linking four together, the fire-rate is almost continuous.'

"You made a machine gun."

"A… what?" she asked.

"Sorry," I replied. "I went back into 21st century-speak again. It's a term that dates back to when multi-fire weapons were first invented.

Nonetheless, it sounds like that could really be a game changer. Too bad we can't mount one on Dora's Remora chassis. Then we'd have air support."

Emily's eyes seemed to glaze over for a minute. She snapped out of it a moment later. "You know, that's a great idea. I'm going to comm the commander and see what he thinks. I probably can't get her ready for tomorrow, but we're still gonna have other battles ahead." She looked off screen for moment. "Okay, I'll be right there."

"Problem?" I said.

"We're still working on mounting our 'machine guns' to the vehicles. There are a few snags but nothing I can't handle. I need to go though."

"All right. Thanks for calling Emily. I do appreciate your worrying about me."

"You take care of yourself Tanner Voss. And be careful tomorrow. We don't want to lose anyone," she grinned. "Not even you."

"Thanks, I think. Voss out."

Chapter Twenty-Four

The morning felt cool and new on my face. The sun had risen only a few moments before, and the auroras weaving across the sky began to fade.

I was in my Mark II with the faceplate up, carrying a large Tripod mount under one arm, and a sizable battery pack under the other. A Dohannen battle rifle was slung crossway over my back and a Ravrath staff weapon hung off the other side. I was ready to rumble.

Chief Moreland, also in armor, led the way carrying the heavy beam cannon while Ensign Ping Teo followed, carrying a crate of Dohannen grenades of some sort. We didn't exactly know what those grenades would do, but we were perfectly willing to lob them at the Ravrath to find out.

Walking at my side, Commander Torvald kept having to break into a trot to keep up with the Mark IIs, as did the Dohannen Irregulars following us. We had a total of six Dohannen. Each of our volunteers was also armed to the teeth, carrying beam-based battle rifles and metal flechette throwing side arms. They were dressed in a variety of not necessarily matching riot and military gear.

Dora had been guiding our group much as she had done for me on my last two excursions into Dangerland, vectoring us around any Rav patrols in our path. We were a fair ways away from the nearest ocean, and the enemy's patrols were not as thick.

Ahead, the Chief signaled for everyone to stop and then motioned for us to go as low as we could. He moved over to a series of thickets, signaling forward of our line of travel, then set the big gun down. We were there.

I lowered my faceplate and my HUD showed highlighted figures through the dirt and rock of the hill, constructs courtesy of Dora's sensor suite. There were thirty Rav infantry and three heavy weapon cars, essentially hover-tanks. I sat the tripod down and Dunar and the chief began assembling our firepower. A few minutes later, I handed Moreland the battery pack and shortly thereafter, the charge monitor on the weapon glowed purple, the Dohannen color for 'good to go.'

The volunteers crawled up to the ridge top, staying low in the knee-high grass. They brought their weapons to bear on our enemy and waited. Ping and I stayed back behind the ridgeline and charged our staff weapons to maximum. Chief Moreland joined us, and Dunar took the small seat on the heavy gun.

"Is this all of them?" Ping asked. "With a little luck, we could have them all down before the other team even attacks. Assuming Dunar can take out the hover tanks."

"I'm afraid it's not that simple, Ensign," Dora said over our comms. "This is just the outer guard. There are another hundred enemy combatants within the facility. Our main advantage is that they think the Dohannen too beaten to ever try to take the power plant back."

"A hundred, eh?" Chief Moreland said. "Plus these thirty, and their heavy guns. We are definitely about to poke the hornet nest. Any other heavy weapons vehicles hiding in there, Dora?"

"One. Though at this time it is powered down and I calculate a ten minute power up cycle."

"In ten minutes," I said, "this could all be over."

"One way or another," said the Chief.

◆

"We're in position, Commander."

"Roger that, Ensign Darkfeather," Torvald replied through his comm. Dora was linking us all, Dohannen and human, into a network. "Dora? You ready to become a gunnery officer?"

"Affirmative, Commander. The Dohannen Vehicles are also self-driving. I've hacked into their navigation suites and am now remote controlling all of them, allowing the flesh and blood soldiers to perform other duties."

"Handy for them. More people to shoulder a rifle instead of sitting behind a wheel. How many vehicles are you fielding in this fight?"

"Seven. I will be sending them, along with their new weapons capabilities first. If we can approach their rear without being noticed, I believe I can cause major havoc before they turn from chasing your section."

"Perfect. Give me a channel to our team, but keep Ensign Darkfeather linked in," He said in a quiet voice. "All right people, we're ready as we're going to be. We shoot when the heavy gun fires, not a moment before. Understood?"

Single mic clicks sounded from everyone. The signal for assent.

Commander Torvald was watching our enemy from Dora's arial view on his padd. "Okay everyone, the three hover tanks are about to converge at the main nexus point for their outside forces. Dunar, I've highlighted that for you. When they get close enough together that they'll get in each other's way you may fire at your discretion. Everyone else, once the heavy gun starts shooting, try to take out as many Rav foot soldiers as you can. However, be ready to turn and run on my signal. No heroics, just head back to the forest as fast as you can go. Clear?"

Multiple mic clicks all around. "Mark IIs? When Dunar starts firing, I want you to use those enhanced strength capabilities of yours to lob as many of those grenades into the midst of the Rav group as you can. Don't stand around and be easy targets, move and throw, throw and move. Clear?"

"Affirmative, Sir," we all replied in unison.

"All good then. Dunar, the show is yours."

While we waited, Ping, the chief and I draped ourselves with bandoliers, each holding about ten grenades. It wasn't going to be the most efficient way to deploy said grenades, but the fingers on a Mark II are surprisingly nimble. Plus, we could throw the weapons about five times as far as an un-enhanced sentient.

"Get ready," Dunar growled from his perch on the heavy gun. "It's time."

The bark from his weapon was much more muted than you'd expect, but the beam was no less deadly. I crested the ridge and began throwing grenades. Below, I could see that one of the Rav hover tanks was billowing smoke, but still seemed to be moving. The Rav around it and the other tanks were scrambling to find us and it didn't take them long.

"Here they come!" Moreland yelled.

The Rav began dashing up the hill as fast as their scoots would take them. This showed me a weakness we should've considered but missed. The scoots slowed down as the grade upward increased. It was the sort of planning error that was actually going in our favor.

The first of our mysterious grenades exploded well above their targets. "Flatten your grenade arcs," Chief Moreland shouted, but it almost wasn't necessary. We'd assumed the grenades were explosive, but they weren't.

They were electrical. Lightning bombs.

"Aim for any groups!" Dunar told us. "The lighting will arc, and their water-filled enviro-armor will conduct it."

We followed his advice, and began to give the Rav a really bad day. That was fine by me, as I watched blasts from the volunteers pierce their armor and our grenades envelope them in minor lightning storms.

You get what you earn.

Unfortunately, once the Rav got over the initial shock, they starting hitting back, hard. Much like soldiers in Earth's revolutionary war of the Americas, they lined up their scoots and formed a firing wall. Their staff weapons simultaneously shot their projectiles at us, and one of our Dohannen Irregulars was hit in the chest. Instead of knocking him unconscious, the shot splattered him across the landscape behind us. The Rav were firing at full power and taking no prisoners this time.

Commander Torvald had crouch-run back to our position, waiting for the signal from the Dohannen military team. As the Rav got closer to us, we were peppering them with beam shots but their intense "broadsides" made all our unarmored people keep their heads down.

Dunar was firing the heavy beamer as quick as its hardware would bring it to full charge again; an interval of roughly sixty seconds. He'd set the first hover tank on fire and he'd somehow managed to hit a second tank right square in it's weapon. It could still maneuver but was effectively useless.

But the third tank had found him.

"Dunar! Get out of there! They're aiming at you!" Chief Moreland yelled, amplified by his suit. Dunar, however, was intensely watching his recharge indicator and looked up in confusion at the chief's warning. He hesitated just a moment too long.

The enemy tank fired what looked like a one of the staff projectiles, though much larger. The result was horrifyingly different. It hit the ridgetop just in front of our heavy gun and exploded with a flash so bright, the polarizer on my faceplate activated. When it dimmed, the thicket, the gun and Dunar were gone. Pieces of twisted metal were the only thing left of the weapon, but there wasn't any part of our gunner left. He'd been vaporized.

Now we knew what we were up against, and it wasn't anything good.

The enemy hover tank began to turn back in our direction, trying to get a shot at our Mark II team when commander Torvald pulled the plug on the operation.

"Fall back! Everyone fall back now! Run!" As one, the Chief, Ping and I dropped our grenades and turned, sprinting as fast as we could from the enemy's field of fire. The Irregulars followed us moving flat out.

"Darkfeather! We're falling back. It's your turn, but watch that remaining tank. Its main cannon is deadly as hell."

Our team fell back to a rock outcropping and waited. We didn't have to wait very long. A roar came from Team two's position, and the sound of beam weapons firing rapid-fire came to us over the ridge top. I switched a side screen on my HUD to Dora's orbital feed and saw multiple smaller vehicles attacking the Rav we'd been fighting from behind. Beams were spitting out in a constant stream of automatic fire from each vehicle, and I saw that each car had more than one multi-shot assembly. The Rav infantry was being decimated, which was just fine by me.

The remaining hover tank however, had enough armor that the multiple-firing small-arms only bounced off its exterior. It turned quickly and lined up on one of Dora's remote attack vehicles and fired. The result was catastrophic. The front half of the vehicle vanished in a flash of coherent energy, leaving the back half flipping end over end. The Rav heavy vehicle was definitely a problem. Dora's vehicles began weaving erratically, all the while continuing their assault on the Rav infantry. She was doing her best, but another of her remote assault cars vanished in a blast of light.

The lack of heavy assault craft for our side looked like it might carry the day against us and probably would have if the Dohannen forces from the Citadel hadn't also been well equipped. We'd had one heavy gun, but they had several and thick beams of light all converged on the enemy hover tank simultaneously. Nanoseconds later, it was no longer a problem.

"They're running!" a voice I recognized as Koabac's came over my comm. "Bottle up the entrance to the plant before they swarm out!"

"Time to move, people," Commander Torvald told us. "Reverse course and let's get ready to ambush the Rav coming out."

We crested the ridge top we'd retreated from, and got our first look at the carnage. Rav lay everywhere, their scoots blasted and their bodies broken. Considering what the Rav had been doing to the Dohannen, I guessed the latter were feeling no small amount of satisfaction. I sure was.

Koabac's forces weren't hesitating at the gate. Led by Dora's remaining assault vehicles, they were storming the Rav positions.

"We're gonna have to sprint to catch Team Two," I said.

"They're fast attacking so that the Rav don't have time to destroy the plant," Moreland replied. He, Ping and I were outpacing Torvald and the Irregulars. Our suits enhanced our speed twice over, and we were getting close to catching our fellow fighters. It was almost a wasted effort.

The Rav hadn't had a chance to swarm out. They'd been clumped up at the entrance, and Dora's assault vehicles had caught them by surprise. The result had been gruesome. From where we were, we'd heard her automatic beam batteries fire, but we'd heard little staff weapon return fire.

When I finally made my way through the gate, the Rav garrison had been wiped out to the last soldier with the exception of a single tank operator who'd been trying to get that weapon powered up. He was the only prisoner taken.

The power plant was ours.

Chapter Twenty-Five

"So Dora, how's tank operator duty suiting you?" Commander Torvald asked.

"Once I infiltrated the enemy computer, which I will admit took a while because of their strange computing infrastructure, I've had no difficulties, Commander," she replied.

"Will you have any problem running a Rav tank and your Dohannen drone vehicles?

"This is far from the first time that I've handled a drone force, as you well know. The battles I've participated in against the Klugg more than prepare me for operating multiple remote combat vehicles. Particularly ones this primitive."

"Okay, Dora. I in no way was questioning your abilities," Torvad said, a slight chuckle in his apology. "Status report?"

"The three assault vehicles I've stationed to protect the personnel at the power plant are well set to provide an ambush to any Rav forces that should try to retake it. Only a concentrated force of enemy hover tanks could manage that, and as you well know, I would see them coming miles away. That would give me more than enough time to activate the... surprises the Dohannen would deploy in such an eventuality."

"Outstanding."

"I have deployed the hover tank at the portal gate, well camouflaged, to cover our retreat when it is time to send everyone through, and deployed my remaining assault craft to patrol the lines between the plant and the gate. The Dohannen in the Citadel are preparing more assault craft with the new weapon configuration for me to take control of when it's time for the inhabitants to transit to the portal."

"I'm beginning to think we're actually going to pull this off," Chief Moreland said.

"Of course, we are," Torvald replied. "But, this brings me to the one snag in our plan. I had intended for Dora to transit back to Hell moon inside Minnie so that she could avoid the discharge effect that knocked us all out. Givall assures me that extra precaution won't be necessary with the gate calculations reconfigured. The problem is though, too much of our plan revolves around defense with the remote vehicles and surveillance from you, Dora. I just don't think we can spare you if this is going to work."

"I see that we are of like minds, Commander," Dora said. "In which case it will need to be someone in a Mark II. Commander, I believe that we both know who it should be."

"Yes, our most junior member, whose suit just happens to be in the worst shape."

"Agreed, Commander," Moreland said. "Voss is the one to go."

"Wait, what?" I said, standing up from the bench I'd been sitting on. "Sir! No! My suit is working fine! You need me here!"

"Someone's gotta do this, Kid," Moreland said. "It's the lynchpin of the whole operation. Commander, I'd also recommend sending Ensign Teo through at the same time for redundancy."

"Hey! Hold on, Chief!" Ping said. "You're gonna need me right here when it all goes down. Another Mark II might make all the difference!"

"Attention!" Torvald barked, and both Ping and I snapped to. "This is not a debate. As it happens, I agree with Chief Moreland. It is more important that word gets back to the *Seeker* and the Captain. If I can get my two most junior people out of harm's way, all the better. You're both going. Understood?"

"Sir! Yes sir!" we both shouted.

"Good. I will put a complete report and all my logs along with annotation provided by Dora on each of your padds. There's no fore-seeable reason why one person couldn't complete your mission but redundancy will guarantee it."

"In the meantime," the Chief said, "I want you both to run full diagnostics on your Mark IIs. Everything needs to be as ship-shape as we can make it, and you're going to need fully working suits when you come out the other side on that sulphurous moon. Understood?"

"Yes Chief!"

"Good. Get to it!"

◆

"This is crazy," I complained. "They're gonna need us. They shouldn't have both of us to go, should they?"

"Maybe not," Ping replied. "But it's the mark of a good senior officer to take any opportunity possible to keep his most junior officers out harm's way. Guess he cares. But seriously, I can see him sending a cadet home, no offense, but I'm fully fledged. He shouldn't be sending me off. I know you could do this without me."

It took all of my willpower not to point out to Ping that she was less than a year out of the academy and chronologically not quite two years older than I was. Not counting my hundred and fifty years of stasis.

"I guess we're stuck with it though," I said. "I'm sure not gonna disobey a direct order."

"Damn straight we're not," she said. "I may be one of the most junior officers on *Seeker*, but I'm not a nut, unlike some people. Which reminds me, Tanner. Word is that you visit the brig every few days to play chess with our terrorist mole. Aside from almost killing us all, she was on a specialized mission to kill you. I mean, what the heck are you thinking?"

I blew out my breath and sat down next to my Mark II. "I realize it's kinda crazy. But she has no one to even talk to, and I kinda feel sorry for her."

"Seriously? I've heard that she thinks you and all the other hybrids on board are devil's spawn meant to destroy mankind."

"Hear me out," I said, perhaps a little too defensively. "She was raised to believe that scrumscuttle every since she was old enough to walk. Earth for Earth is a fanatic organization and it shouldn't be any surprise that someone raised by them would be a fanatic."

"Yeah. I got that she's a nut job."

"But when she forgets that she's a fanatic, she's actually a decent person. Don't get me wrong, I'd never trust her outside her cell, but... she's just been used as a tool all her life. I.. I just feel sorry for her."

"All right, Cadet Pureheart, but if she ever tries to wheedle any favors out of you, you come see Auntie Ping and I will whack you on the back of your pointy little head until common sense prevails. Promise me. That woman is nothing but trouble for you and all the rest of us. Promise."

"I promise, Auntie."

"That's my good little cadet," She said. "How's your Mark II look? Diagnostics finished?"

"Everything's green, even the replaced knee hardware," I patted my banged-up armor. "Man, imagine if we hadn't had these when we came here."

"We'd have been dead. Remember what condition we were in when we got here. I sure hope that Givall's recalcs have solved all those problems."

"Hey, he has Dora, Torvald and Emily on his side, as well as Lalall. It's gonna be fine. I hope."

"I sure hope so, too," she said. "We've got a crap-ton of civilians to get through the gate, most without any kind of armor. It has to work or the whole thing goes to rubbish. So many moving parts to this plan, we'd better keep our fingers crossed."

Chapter Twenty-Six

It was another gorgeous dawn, just like it had been a few days before. It had taken the rest of the previous day to get power to the system and get a console of Givall's devising to the portal we'd come through.

Several Dohannen troops surrounded the area. I was standing before the gate with Ping, while Chief Moreland did a final systems check on our Mark IIs. Givall, Lalall and Commander Torvald stood at the makeshift control panel for the gate, making last minute adjustments and calculations. Torvald walked over to us.

"Remember, you should emerge only a few minutes after we originally left, but these calculations are very 'fiddly' and you may have a little more time elapse than we're planning on. I guarantee that it won't be more than a day after we entered the portal, nor will you have to worry about landing there before we left. I shudder to think of the paradox we'd make if that happened, so we've built in a little padding on the calculations to make sure it doesn't."

"We're ready, Sir," Ping told him. "We've both got copies of all the logs and data, plus your personal report to the Captain. We won't let you down."

"I never considered for a moment that you would, Ensign," Torvald said, smiling. "Either of you. Once you get through, Chief Moreland has made some enhancements to your comms to call the ship. If that doesn't work, get to the shuttle and contact *Seeker*. Make sure your reports go to the Captain, and give them our calculations on transferring the gate to the surface. They should be able to stabilize its matrix and move it with the grapple field.

"Understood," Ping told him.

"The calculations should also allow them to connect with this time period and we can then get the Dohannen through to the future. If all goes right, you two should return here within a few days of leaving, thought it may take a while for you to get things set up in the *Seeker's* time. The delay will give us time to get everything ready on this end."

"I sure hope there's not some hidden catch to moving forward in time, Commander," I said. "Hopefully we won't crumble to dust or something."

"Very unlikely, Cadet. That's more the realm of fantasy and magic than science. Hopefully." He looked at the gate, then back to us. "All right, you two. Time to suit up and get this show on the road."

I stepped into my Mark II and sealed it up. Once my faceplate lowered, my HUD lit up and the suit did a quick sys-check. All systems were green but I knew this suit would need a full overhaul once back on the Seeker.

"I'm green and good to go," I said.

"Same here," Ping said through comms.

"Givall, Lalall, it's time to make this work," Torvald told the Do-hannen scientists. "Fire it up."

A few moments later, the dimensions of the gate became fluid and the gate itself began to glow with a purplish aura. A silvery veil now covered the event horizon. All that was left was for us to step through.

I looked over at Ping, and she gave me a thumbs up which I returned. She and I stepped forward then into the gate and hopefully, back to the future.

◆

I'd been unconscious the first time we'd gone though the gate. Having been assured this time would be easier, I had some expectations for this trip. I was quite wrong.

I'd expected to be one moment on the planet Susanowo, and the next to be on the moon Hell but I watched the timer on my HUD slow to a crawl. My perception seemed normal, but time itself seemed to be ready to stop completely. For a moment I wondered if we'd gone into another universe where we'd be trapped forever.

At times like this, my mind is able to conjure a wide variety of possible but unlikely disasters. My sister Valiel claimed that this was my super-power. She may have been right.

I could hear my heartbeat, and it seemed it was beating once every ten minutes. One would think that if your physiology slowed down this far, so would your perception. I wasn't able to see anything except a silvery mirror that reflected nothing.

The next moment, we were through. My vision cleared as the gate seemed to spit us out with a small amount of forward momentum. Slightly ahead of me, I could see Ping stumble and drop to one knee. I wondered if she felt as dizzy and nauseous as I did.

As the dizziness cleared, I was able to take in our surroundings. It was definitely the sulfurous moon Hell we'd wound up on. Hopefully, we were only a few minutes from the time we'd been originally sent through.

I looked down, and saw where Minnie the Miner's treads had been sitting, near the gate. I couldn't gauge how much time had passed because the energetic/magnetic field around the gate's functioning had again disturbed the chemical laden dust. Around us, the bones of the unfortunate Dohannen who'd come to the wrong place were still exposed.

"The gate's still with us," Ping said, looking behind us.

"Did you notice it didn't feel like being disassembled this time?" I asked.

"Yeah. Much smoother. Let's get to the shuttle. Two of the K-bots are still here and unpowered, lets each carry one back with us while we're at it."

She picked up K-16 while I grabbed K-21 and we started the journey to our ride off this ghastly place. It was not a long trudge, but the very harshness of our environment made it seem to take forever. Eventually, a lull in the caustic winds showed the shape of the shuttle.

"Never been so glad to see our ride as this," I said as Ping signaled the aft hatch to open.

"Hell yeah," she replied. "Let's get a signal to *Seeker* and get this info where it needs to be. You pilot, Tanner. You need the practice."

"Uh… you sure? I mean…"

"I have every confidence in you, Cadet. Get it done."

"You sound like you're channeling the chief, Ensign," I said while divesting myself of my Mark II. Performing the pre-flight took a little longer than it probably took most pilots, but I was determined not to flub up in any way.

"Looks like we're green," Ping said. "I was a little worried. The atmosphere here is nothing you want to leave your machinery sitting out in very long. Once we're clear of the moon, I'll send a call out to the ship."

We rose from the surface in a cloud of dust and I set a course outbound from the moon. A few minutes later, we'd cleared Hell's influence and Ping signaled to the *Seeker*. While she did that, I used the shuttle's sensor suite to get a fix on the ship.

"Ping, I am not picking up *Seeker* on my scans. Where the heck are they?"

"I'm not getting a response, either. Oh, this is not good."

"We need to find them! Emily..er.. Ensign Darkfeather and all the rest are counting on us!"

"Stay frosty, Tanner. Remember, they are half a million years in the past. It doesn't so much matter how fast we get to them, as much as it is simply that we do get to them at the right moment in time. From what I understand, we could take a year to get this going and still emerge five minutes after we left."

"Right. I'm cool. Everything's cool. But… what if the calculations are off, or are somehow dependent on when we head back there? I'd hate to arrive a day too late."

"We're going as fast as we can. I'm getting a response from our surface group. Hello Commander M'Buku! This is Ensign Teo. Sir, we have information for the captain that is Alpha Priority! Where is the *Seeker*, sir?"

M'Buku's visage appeared on the small comm screen in front of us. "The hull plating, as you probably know Ensign, was near completion when you and your team went to that moon. It was finished while you were there and the Captain decided to perform the jump drive test ahead of schedule. *Seeker* is out of the system, but I can get a message to the ship via our long range tranceiver and the Remora probes which have stationed themselves along her route. What is this priority message?"

"Sir, it's a very long story. A good half a million years long. Permission to join you on the surface to make our report?"

"Granted. Land as soon as possible. You have intrigued me Ensign. Make haste."

"Aye, sir," Ping said, looking over at me and gesturing toward the controls, "we'll see you shortly."

◆

I had barely set the shuttle down, when Ping, out of her Mark II and wearing only her rumpled uniform, had the hatch open. Commander M'Buku, *Seeker's* first officer was waiting to meet us. Ping was giving him her report almost before her feet touched down on Susanowo's soil.

It took us a good twenty minutes to give even an overview of what had happened to us and through most of it the Commander's expression was one of concerned amazement. He then listened to Commander Torvald's more comprehensive version residing on Ping's padd.

"So you're telling me," he said, looking up from Torvald's report, "that not only did we miss the signs of not one, but two advanced past civilizations, but also any signs of an energetic gateway to another time and place? You astonish me!"

"Yes sir," I said. "I can only guess that the remains of these ancient people's world has degraded to the point that our Remoras took said remains as natural formations. At this point, even the continents are different."

"But, sir," Ping said. "There is a plan of action to get not only our people, but the remains of the Dohannen civilization back here with them."

"Damn it," M'Buku said. "Torvald, Darkfeather and Carstairs

should have come back with you. There is an entire ethical dilemma around changing the past but now, there's no choice."

I wondered to myself if Commander Torvald had engineered events so that there was no room for M'Buku or the captain to make the choice to get our team out and leave the past as it was: ie leaving the Dohannen swinging in the wind. My respect for Torvald, already pretty high, soared to new heights. Ping's complete lack of expression at M'buku's complaint made me believe she probably felt the same.

"At any rate," M'Buku said, "we need to get our captain in the loop. Come with me, you two. We need to fire up the long range comms."

Chapter Twenty-Seven

Five hours later, the *E.S.S. Seeker* was back in orbit and M'Buku, Ping and I were on board and standing in front of the captain in her office.

"Oh do sit down," she said. "Going over these reports, this is some of the most fantastic information I think anyone has ever seen. If I didn't trust Torvald so much, I'd almost think a couple of junior officers were indulging in some sort of ill-advised joke."

Ping and I looked at each other with a worried expression, and Captain Yamashita chuckled. "Don't worry kids. I believe what I'm seeing. It seems our primary goals are going to have to be getting our people and these… Dohannen… back to this time period all in one piece."

"So," M'Buku said, "we are committing to bringing this group back to what is essentially their future? I definitely have concerns on what the consequences of that might be, Captain."

The captain looked up from the report she was reading. "I've read enough on the subject of this sort of thing in both theoretical science and popular fiction to know there are dozens of theories on how this could go, Ingoye. The truth being that they are all just theories. I look at this world as it is now, with no higher life forms and can't help but wonder how could things have turned out worse for their civilizations? I also can't really see how it could effect us, since this world has been isolated and alone for millennia upon millennia."

"With the Dohannen gone, Ma'am, these Ravrath could conceivably become dominant. We might wind up with a changed world where they've taken over and in the process, lose Earth's first probable colony world."

"Ma'am," Ping said from the couch where we'd both landed, "at this point, the Ravrath already are the dominant species. The number of Dohannen we want to bring back is less than twenty thousand. That is the last remainder of a civilization that numbered over a billion people. If we hadn't shown up, they would've been taken to extinction by the Rav. All we're doing is removing them from that equation early."

"And with less extinction," I chimed in, belatedly remembering who I was talking to. 'Er.. Ma'am."

"I tend to agree," the captain said, looking back down at Torvald's report. "We'll do our best to bring these people into the twenty-third century. However, from these schematics and adjustments we'll need to make, we should get started on moving that gate with all possible haste."

◆

I wasn't really involved with the planning process of getting the gate from the moon to Susanowo's surface. Ping and I were assigned to the tender mercies of Master Chief Kurakin, my academy mentor and head of security for the *Seeker*. The six foot two valkyrie, with her colorless grey eyes and cropped blond hair looked the part and no junior officer would've dared be flip with her, NCO or not.

"The captain has decided 'in for a penny, in for a pound' on this adventure," she said from the head of the conference table. We were surrounded by the entire fifteen person security team for the ship and I was sure that Ping felt as intimidated as I did.

"We're here to answer any questions that we can, Chief," Ping said. "Tanner and I have fought these fishy bastards and I'm hoping that we can be useful to you."

"I'm sure you will be, Ma'am," Kurakin replied as Ping technically outranked her. Everyone knew that the Master Chief was merely being polite. "The captain has authorized me to take most of my team though in our Godzilla suits. If you two can give us an idea of what our opponents are using and how they fight, we can decide what kind of load-out to arm our armor with."

"Do we have any scan data on these fish people?" Corporal McKeown asked. McKeown was a native of New Zealand and put a lot of time in the gym. He looked like he could use me as a dumbbell to tone up his biceps, and I'm over six foot and weigh near 200 pounds.

Big guy.

"As it happens we do," Kurakin said, firing up the table's holo-projector. "Aside from a lot of scans from both our guests Mark IIs and scans from Dora the Remora, we also have helmet cam footage from the battle for the power plant that was a joint op between our people and the Dohannen military."

"Sweet," Private Hodgekins said. She was a native of the North American country of Canada and unlike McKeown, she would barely come up to my chest height-wise. However, she was built like an Olympic gymnast and had a reputation for sending her fellow security people to the infirmary when sparring sessions got a little too heated. "I look forward to the intel, but if these kids… er, no offense ma'am," she nodded to Ping, "but if they can do this much damage to these jerks with engineering suits, we could probably take over the damn planet with our Godzillas."

"Like the enthusiasm," Kurakin said. "But lets not get overconfident. I've reviewed the battle footage and these 'Rav' have tanks with some sort of cannon that looks like it could take one of our armored suits out with a single shot. Our core mission isn't about smashing the fish people, this is a rescue mission. We want to get our people and these Dohannen, who appear to be ancestors to the Medegin, back to our side of this portal. This is most likely a 'covering a retreat' scenario."

"Long as we get to see some action in our suits," Hodgekins said. "When the bots on *Seeker* all went nuts, we didn't even have time to suit up before some killjoy shut them all down!"

Kurakin looked at Hodgekins for a moment as if worrying about her sanity, then returned to the topic at hand. "I want everyone to review the attached files. We'll meet back here at 14:00 sharp and formulate a final plan of action. Ensign, Cadet, we'll want you here then. It's more likely we'll have pertinent questions after everyone has all the facts." She stood, and everyone else followed suit.

"Dismissed!"

Chapter Twenty-Eight

It took a good three days to formulate plans, and to make the necessary adjustments to the shuttles and *Seeker* for our grappling fields to be able to move the gate.

The first step, getting it off the surface of Hell moon was not that difficult. Our two largest shuttles flanked the gate while the *Seeker* orbited above it. All three engaged their fields simultaneously and between them, the Dohannen edifice lifted with no complications into a stationary orbit above the moon.

Ping and I, since we were so deeply involved with the entire affair got to ride in one of the shuttles as spectators. The actual piloting was done by the best pilots the ship had. Junior engineering officers were just along on a courtesy ride.

Lieutenant Jim Fowler, our shuttle pilot, was the 2nd shift helm officer on *Seeker*. We were in the starboard side shuttle to the gate, and Jim was tasked with keeping one side of the stabilizing trinity in just the right place.

"Well," he said, "we've got her into space, now comes the hard part. Getting her down safely on Susanowo."

"It seemed pretty smooth getting it out here," I said.

"Oh yeah," Fowler replied, "but now, not only do we have to deal with increased gravimetric shear, but we also have to deal with actual planetary weather. Also, *Seeker* is going to be damn low in the atmosphere, and while she's rated for planetary landings she handles like a wounded whale this deep into the gravity well. This'll definitely be tricky, so no distractions please. Ensign Teo? How are we looking on the grapples?"

"Five by five, sir. Well within energetic parameters."

Fowler keyed our comm. "Assault shuttle, how are things looking on your side?" The security force's shuttle, heavily armored and designed for emergency extractions of crew members from difficult situations, was our second most powerful shuttle after the cargo shuttle that we currently rode in.

"We are looking good and green over here, Lieutenant. *Seeker* is signaling they are ready to start descent on your mark."

"Roger that, Fowler out. *Seeker*, this is cargo one. We are ready to descend. On my signal, we begin the operation. And… mark." Fowler hit a switch on the control giving everyone the green light and we began our long trip into Susanowo's atmosphere.

Rather than dropping down, we took the gate on a long winding path to a spot halfway around the planet, a pre-planned destination. Even as careful as we were being, winds buffeted the craft, while rain almost whited out the view ports. I was extremely glad to not be at the helm.

At last, we broke into clear weather and I could see the continent we were aiming for ahead. I took a quick walk to the back of the shuttle, and looking through the rear view port, I could see the massive back half of the *Seeker* above us, trailing a plume of icy condensation. It was strange seeing her against the bright blue sky with its tatters of borealis displays. I'd only ever seen her against the backdrop of space.

I was nearly taken off my feet when the shuttle gave a hard bounce. It took every once of self control I had not to blurt out "what happened?"

"Damn!" Fowler said. "The weather having more of an effect than we estimated."

"It shouldn't be affecting these big shuttles that much!" Ping said.

"It's not the shuttles, it's the huge donut-shaped brick we're towing. Cadet! Get to your seat and strap in."

I did so, and was glad of it a moment later when our shuttle tipped forty-five degrees toward the side the gate was on.

"*Seeker*, I need for you to pull in closer and stabilize our flight path," Fowler said. The shaking and bumping lessened.

Minutes later, I could make out individual trees as we made our final approach and we set the gate down with an anti-climactic thud that resonated through the shuttle. Looking out my nearest port, I could see the *Seeker* arcing back upward into the sky. We'd done it.

The gate was in position. Now the question was, could we make it work on our end?

◆

A day later, two large fusion generators stood fifty yards back from each side of the portal. Givall's reports had made it quite clear that the portal only worked one way at a time. If we wanted to go to them, we needed to power it on our end. If they wanted to come to us, they needed it powered on their end.

Ping and I were standing next to two different Mark II suits, the ones we'd been using before having been pulled for full refurbishment. It had taken a great deal of persuading on our part to get the Captain to allow us to go back with the security team. Our pleas had gone unheeded until Chief Kurakin had stepped in to assure the Captain that A: our experience with the situation would indeed come in useful, and that B: she would guarantee our safety.

Master Chief Kurakin rarely guaranteed anything unless she was dead sure of it. Captain Yamashita relented.

Our armor stood in the middle of a formation surrounded by the Security Operations team's 'Godzilla' suits. The Mark IIs made us look pretty damn big, but the Godzillas made our engineering suits look like we were driving small sports sedans in comparison. The heavily shielded security armor was covered with various boxy bits, extensions and tubes, all of which hid assorted weapons of mayhem and destruction. You only used this armor when you were up a certain creek and needed a very destructive paddle.

"How are you two doing?" First Officer M'Buku asked, walking between the forest of armor all around us. "I'd be surprised if you didn't have some butterflies in your stomachs over going back there."

"We are green to go sir!" I said.

"I know that we'll be an asset to the mission, Commander," Ping told him.

"I have no doubt of that," M'Buku replied. "I am not going to lie though. The calculations for your arrival are to the minute five days after you left the past. A lot can happen in five days. But if something's happened to the gate back there, we'll know in a few minutes. If we can't connect with it, the mission is scrubbed."

Ping and I watched the technicians at our makeshift portal control nervously. If we couldn't get the gate to work, everyone we'd left in the past was on a road to extermination. It had to work, but... it was time travel. I couldn't begin to conceive of the possible variables. If our calculations missed something, or the Rav had somehow taken the portal on their end...

"Commander, Sec Ops is ready to enter and energize our armor," Chief Kurakin said, walking up to us. "I'll initiate our combat link net as soon as we're buttoned up."

"Don't let me delay you then, Chief," M'buku said. He looked over toward the technicians, and one of them gave him the thumbs up. "Looks like we're ready to try this, everyone. So once the portal is engaged remember the plan, and good luck to you all."

"All right, ladies and gentlemen, time to use our power for good," Kurakin yelled out. "Suit up and energize. Check comms once you are green. That includes you too, Ensign, Cadet."

I climbed into my Mark II, ran the sys-check and keyed into the command net the security team had initiated. I listened as each team member reported in, and when my number came up, so did I. The twelve of us who were going though the portal moved up, Ping and I in the center of the group, and waited for the gate to activate. To each side of the portal, two more very disappointed people in Godzilla suits waited to cover our retreat in case any of the Ravs tried to follow us back into the present. The only ones more disappointed were the three security people who'd been left on Seeker to watch things up there.

"Captain," M'Buku said into his comm, "We are ready to give it a try."

"Proceed Commander," Captain Yamashita said from her chair on *Seeker's* bridge. Regulations specified in most operations that the captain would remain aboard. This generally put the XO in the thick of things when command had to be established for exploratory landings and such. M'Buku wouldn't be going through with us, but he'd be coordinating everything on this end.

He nodded to the two technicians and they began working the console.

"Initializing." The lead tech said. "Increasing power flow, and here we go!"

There was no large energetic display. One moment we were looking though the ring of the portal at the landscape beyond, the next the portal surrounded a mirror finish we couldn't see through.

"Heads up everyone," Kurakin's voice came over comms. "We go through four abreast, sixty second intervals. Once through, move out of the way so the next people can come through. We'll do a head count once on the other side in case any of you get lost on the way."

"Lost?" Hodgekins voice said. "Is she kidding, Tanner?"

"Yeah. There's no getting lost unless somehow we all screw up. The transmission seems like it takes a while because your perception is changed, but the pass through is less than ten seconds."

"Form up!" Kurakin said. We all moved into prearranged positions and waited. "All right. It's go time!" The first line in our formation stepped through and vanished. Ping and I waited sixty seconds then stepped up and through.

The time disorientation was the same. My brain was faster than my physiology. If the Dohannen were all ready to go on the other side, we could start cycling them through, back to the Seeker's side immediately. Hopefully before the Rav ever knew we were leaving. That was the plan.

Of course, plans rarely survive contact with the enemy.

Chapter Twenty-Nine

I completed the step I'd started five hundred thousand years in the future, emerging in the planet's past. Before I even checked on my surroundings, I made sure to move out and to the side of the gate to leave room for those behind me.

Having done that, I took stock of what was around me. Commander Torvald, Chief Moreland, Givall and Lallal were all walking toward us from Givall's console. The two Dohannen children Zatta and Kipo, were sticking close to Lallal. Some traveling bags were stacked near the console.

Kurakin and her first line people were in front of us, Ping was next to me, and Sgt. Ameer was on her right. Private Hodgekins was to my left and I could feel the final line stepping out behind us. Everyone was here.

Except the Dohannen. And Dr. Carstairs and Emily Darkfeather. Evidently, the plan had fallen apart on this end.

Chief Kurakin had opened her face plate. "Commander! Where are the civilians? This was supposed to be a grab and go operation."

"I'm afraid we've had some big complications, Master Chief," Torvald said, worry evident on his face. "But, am I glad to see you. I think you'll be able to take care of our complications with those techo-terrors you're wearing."

"What's the SNAFU, sir?"

"The problem is that we seriously underestimated how long it would take to get over twenty thousand undisciplined non-military men, women and children from the Citadel to this plain. The other problem is that the Ravrath caught on to what was happening pretty early, and Dora reports that they're sending a large force to intercept our people."

Kurakin almost rubbed the bridge of her nose in frustration, but realized she was about to do so with a big armored claw-hand. I heard Private Hodgekins mutter, "Excellent!"

"We need to get to them ASAP," Kurakin said. "Who knows the route? Ensign Teo? Tanner?"

"Dora can overlay a vector on your HUDs, but she's very busy right now running the Dohannen's robotic attack vehicles. Tanner's done the route multiple times."

"All right. Jenkins, Steranko, you stay here to secure the gate. The rest of you, minus Ensign Teo…" Ping tried to protest. "Sorry Ensign, essential personnel only. We'll need you here to help coordinate when we get thousands of civvies trying to get through the gate. A stampede could be as dangerous to them as the fish faces. Everyone else, form up on Voss, and keep in mind that engineering suit moves slower than the Godzillas. I only want to be keeping tabs on one person. Tanner, lead the way."

I started out in the direction of the Citadel. "Mom? Are you able to give me any kind of vector to their position?"

Dora's voice came from my helmet comm. She sounded stressed. "I can give you a generalized path, Tanner, but as you may have guessed, I'm very busy at this particular moment. The Rav have strengthened their individual infantry armor and they are killing my vehicles much quicker that expected. Get Chief Kurakin and her team here as quickly as possible."

"We're on our way!" I started sprinting, and the fact that I had a brand new Mark II on sent me dashing across the landscape. I was going much faster than the average sentient could go unaided, but looking in one of my rear-view cams, I could see the security people in their Godzillas were slowing down so as not to pass me.

Even with the lesser speed of my suit, we seemed to fly over the landscape. All the times I'd made the trip before, I'd been doing my best to move slow and be stealthy, now, there was no need. It was balls to the wall, full frontal attack. In less than ten minutes, we came abreast of the leading edge of the Dohannen civilian column. I looked over, and saw a petite figure waving.

"Go *Seeker!*" Ensign Emily Darkfeather practically screamed from her position at a gunner seat on a Dohannen heavy personnel carrier. "Blast 'em back to the depths!"

Things were fairly sedate at the head of the column, but became more and more chaotic as we went farther along. I saw wounded Dohannen laying across the hoods of vehicles in makeshift stretchers and injured people being helped along by their fellow refugees. The Rav had made their mark back here.

"These civilians are too strung out," Kurakin said. "I can hear battle sounds ahead. The Rav must be harassing the rear of the column."

A few moments later, we got to see the problem. The rear of the column mostly consisted of the remaining Dohannen security forces and frankly, they were getting the hell beat out of them. I had expected a large number of Ravrath to try and stop the prey from escaping, but I hadn't expected the horde that confronted us. There were thousands of the enemy on their scoots, and one of the things likely saving the Dohannen so far was that the small mobility scooters that the Rav infantry were using not only helped their movement but also hindered them in that they invariably were getting in each other's way.

The Ravs were trying to get close enough to the Dohannen to take them alive with the lower power setting of their staff weapons. The only thing slowing them from achieving this was a small group of robotic Dohannen vehicles with the battle rifle clusters that Emily had come up with. Dora was doing the best she could, but I saw that the Rav infantry had definitely gotten better armor over their environmental suits. It took multiple battle rifle shots to take a soldier down.

"They've got tanks," McKeown said. "I count fifteen. Suggest we concentrate on them first, Chief."

"Good call. All Godzillas, activate Stingers. I am designating targets. On my signal, fire on the tank I've painted for you. Hopefully we can take out some of their infantry with collateral damage. Follow up with plasma grenades. Weapons free everyone."

The Rav hadn't really taken notice of the new players on the field. Their hover tanks were decimating Dora's robotic forces, and doing their best to keep between her assault vehicles and the more vulnerable infantry. There were only four robotics left and as we watched, one of the Rav tanks vaporized most of another one.

"All Sec Ops, you have green light to fire," Kurakin said.

Almost simultaneously fiery plumes of death lanced out from fold-out launchers on the armored security suits. The Stinger missiles were a far cry from the hand-held launched weapons of my 21st century. The programable yield warheads on the tiny missiles used energy dispersal explosions instead of the chemical explosives of my age. Consequently they could go from explosions the size of a hand grenade to ones the size of a city block, depending on how they were programed to explode.

Evidently, no one on our security team had a great deal of sympathy for the Rav. Eight enemy tanks, along with several of the ground troops using them for cover, disappeared in massive flashes of light and heat.

"Reload second missile!" Kurakin said, some urgency in her voice.

Looking toward the enemy, I saw that the Rav were well aware of us now. The remaining tanks were turning to draw a bead on the team's mobile armor.

"Suggest we charge and close with the infantry, Ma'am," Hodgekins called out. "Maybe they won't shoot if we're in among their troops."

"Roger that!" Kurakin replied. "Everyone, charge the infantry. Set plasma cannons to auto and wade in. Voss! Stick close so the tanks can't bullseye you!"

The Godzillas began sprinting and leaping toward the lines of Rav soldiers advancing on us and it was everything I could do to stay close to Kurakin's six. Without thought, I jerked to one side just before a flash went past my head, and I realized I'd just missed being vaporized by one of the enemy tank's turret blasts. I increased my speed even more.

I reached the front line just in time to see how badly outmatched the Rav infantry were compared to the Sec Ops team. It was a slaughter. The automatic plasma throwers were much stronger than the Dohannen battle rifles and went through the Rav's new armor like it wasn't there. The enemy infantry became a jumbled mess as the soldiers in front tried to turn their scoots around to flee and ran into the ones following them.

A terrible flash appeared down the line from Kurakin and I. The enemy tanks, deciding that their infantry was expendable, had fired at us. One of the Godzillas near was on its side and pouring smoke out between the joints.

"Concentrate Stingers on the remaining tanks!" Kurakin barked out. "Voss! Hodgekins is down. I'm remote opening her armor, peel her out of there and high-tail it back to the column. Move, Mister!"

I dashed over the smoking remains of Rav soldiers, and prayed one of the enemy tanks wasn't lining me up for a kill-shot.

"Mom? Can you get any vitals from Hodgekins?"

"She is alive," Dora said, "though her readings are fluctuating. Definitely unconscious. Chief Kurakin has cracked her suit's access hatch, but it is jammed. You will need to employ brute force to get her out of there. Caution is advised."

"Definitely good advice in this situation," I replied as a small horde of Stinger missiles passed over me. I reached the downed Godzilla suit and saw the damage. Having seen the destructive capabilities of the enemy tanks, it was a testament to the Godzilla suit designers that its shield had deflected a good portion of the attack. Even with that, I could see it was a write off, with one of the legs half melted and an arm missing. I was glad for the safety features that had kept Hodgekins own arsenal from cooking off and finishing the job.

Her suit was lying face down, which was fortunate for me. I thought I'd be able to lift it if I had to with my Mark II, but I wasn't sure. Looking down at her back, I could see that Hodgekins armored hatch had tried to open, but jammed leaving only a slight gap.

This wasn't a problem. The security armor was configured to stop force coming in, not pulling outward. Gripping the hatch with my gauntlets, I crouched and then heaved, doing most of the lifting with my legs.

Something broke inside, then something else and the hatch assembly swung open. I could see Hodgekins, and she didn't look good. She had a singed look on one side of her face and blood was leaking from her ears and nose. I decided to not try and strip her out of her harnesses, and simply tore the entire pilot assembly loose to pull her out. I picked the unit up, and began my fastest pace, burdened as I was, back to the Dohannen column.

"This is Voss. I have Private Hodgekins and am bugalooing out of here. Would appreciate any cover fire you folks can give me."

"Copy," Kurakin said. "McKeown, cover Voss and follow him back to the column. Sec Ops group. We will all begin to fall back in one hundred twenty seconds from my mark. Mark!"

I ran as fast as I could go and still avoid giving Hodgekins a rough ride. Flipping to my rear view camera, I could see one of the Godzilla suits move in behind me, it's plasma weapon turning 180 degrees on its shoulder mounts and firing to the rear at targets of opportunity.

I had only gotten a short way when I felt my danger sense go off big time. I dropped to one knee and did my best to shield Hodgekins as one of the deadly bolts from a hover tank turret passed over me. It was close enough that my shields flared brightly around me.

"Jesus!" McKeown called out over comms. "Can someone put the hurt on that last tank? It's got a clean shot at us!"

"Anyone have stingers left?" Kurakin called out. All responses were negative.

"Chief," I said, resuming my run, "They're not that stable. If you can get close, you can probably flip it."

"Sec team, advance at full speed on that tank. Stay evasive and don't let it get a bead on you."

I set my right rear camera to watch the enemy craft. It began to spin, trying to line up on the rapidly approaching security team. The base would spin one way, while the turret swiveled the other but it was no use. When the first Godzilla landed on the tank's port side, the Rav vehicle noticeably listed to port. When the second security team member landed next to the first, the tank was immobilized and half turned over. Two more armored figures approached the starboard side and began lifting.

"James! Nakamura! When we lift, you jump and jet." Kurakin was one of the suits on the starboard side. "Now!"

The port siders jumped straight up, firing their thrusters at the same time. The starboard siders yanked upward. The result was one upside down tank, essentially unable to put up any kind of fight. As the team moved away from it, Kurakin fired a few plasma grenades into its cannon mount and underside anti-grav assembly. Even if the Rav could flip it back over, it'd be useless in the fight.

All of the security team broke away and followed McKeown and I, their own weapons firing behind them.

"Looks like we've broken their advance," McKeown said. "They're not following us."

"Yet," I said. "We all know the stakes here."

"Yes," Kurakin replied. "And my guess is that if those foot soldiers fail to secure the Dohannen and us to feed to their giant fish god, said foot soldiers will be the first of the Rav to be sent down its gullet."

"That's some definite motivation," Private Nakamura chimed in. "Hopefully the pounding we just gave 'em will cool their desire to be right on our heels."

"I've got one thing that'll cool their ardor," Kurakin said. "Dora, can you remote scuttle Hodgekins armor?"

"I was just about to suggest doing so, Chief. The Ravrath are swarming over it, and bringing up some sort of anti-gravity sled to load it on. I assume they want to reverse engineer it."

"Perfect. Blow it, and make sure to leave a big crater."

My external microphone picked up a large 'boom' behind us and a quick switch to rear view confirmed a small mushroom cloud rising above the hillside behind us.

"Holy cats!" Private James exclaimed. "Dora, how'd you get an explosion that big? I didn't know these suits could go up like that."

"I overloaded the fusion power plant and all of the suit's plasma ammunition simultaneously, Private. It's an old trick used by the Laldoralin military AIs when our AI controlled fighting units were too damaged to continue to be useful."

"Damn. Glad you're on our side, Dora."

"She gets that a lot," I said.

◆

I was still carrying Hodgekins frame even though we'd managed to catch up with the tail end of the Dohannen column. The security team had spread out in a fan shape behind us, watching for the Rav to make their next play.

I was carrying the private still because there was literally no room on any of the vehicles. Each Dohannen transport was filled to over-capacity with the injured, with children and men and women who were unable to keep up. Part of the reason we were so far behind schedule is that half the population of the citadel was on foot, walk-ing beside the vehicles.

"This is insane," The Dohannen medic riding on my shoulder said as she did her best to render first aid to Hodgekins. I was helping her maintain her balance with one of the tool extenders from my suit's right arm as she reached into the pilot cage I carried. "This being needs an actual medical facility."

"Mom?" I asked over comms. "How far are we from the portal? These people have been living underground for the past few years. The ones walking are starting to look pretty ragged."

"The leading edge of the column is approximately 2.13 miles from the entrance to the gate. At your current rate of speed, barely two miles per hour, I estimate that we will be able to start sending people through in just over two hours."

"Chief," I said, calling Kurakin, "Maybe we should send all the transports on ahead."

"I was thinking along similar lines," she replied. "With this many people, there's going to be a logjam. Probably be in everyone's best interests if we can stagger the groupings going to the other side."

"Roger that." I connected to Emily Darkfeather in the lead ve-hicle. "Em? It's Tanner. The Chief and I think it would be a good idea if you took the transports ahead and started sending everyone through that you can carry."

"But that will leave you without the fire support from our defensive weaponry, Tanner. I can't leave you and the Sec Ops people swinging in the wind like that."

"We can fend for ourselves quite nicely, Ensign," Chief Kurakin cut in. "You need to get as many of these people to the gate as you can carry. Cram them in, stack them like cordwood, I don't care. It's only two miles. I've talked to Torvald, and the gate is ready to fire up when he and the scientists see the whites of your eyes."

"Understood," Darkfeather said. Her voice switched from my comms to loudspeaker mounted on the first transport. "Everyone listen. If you are walking, and having trouble keeping up, then you need to climb on a transport. I don't care if you're standing on someone's feet or sitting in their lap. People in the transports, it's about to get extra uncomfortable in there, but we're almost to the gate. Everyone who is in good shape, you'll still be walking but maybe a little faster. We'll all meet on the other side, if the Universe is willing."

The Marx brothers style fire-drill of getting more people on the trucks took several minutes, but shortly thereafter the vehicles sped up and left the column behind.

"Dora," Kurakin said, "How many of your remote vehicles are left?"

"Out of fifty-three, I have two still operational, though one of these has lost all its weaponry. I was going to use it as a battering ram."

"Actually, that's perfect. Bring your toothless car up. Voss. I want you to load Hodgekins and her medic on that vehicle and send them ahead. The faster Private Hodgekins is through that gate, the faster she can get access to *Seeker's* medical personnel."

One of the robotic assault vehicles came tearing up toward us and slewed sideways to a stop. It was scorched, and it's weapons had effectively been stripped away, but it was still mobile. I set both Hodgekins and her medic down for a moment, and moving to the vehicle, I tore the roof away as carefully a I could. Picking up Vanessa Hodgkins' pilot core, I gingerly set it in the back of the car while the medic climbed into the front.

"See you in the future," I told her. "We'll be along presently."

"Good luck to you all," The medic said, and then the vehicle took off ahead of us and was soon lost to sight. Looking around, there were still a large number of seemingly able-bodied Dohannen walking with us. Much to my surprise, I recognized one of them as he approached.

"Krell! You made it."

"That remains to be seen, Guppy. Heard you got swallowed and lived to tell the tale, which I definitely want to hear about when we're all safe."

"Why are you walking, Krell? No offense, but you're no guppy yourself. You could've ridden on one of the transports and almost be on your way out of here."

The old Dohannen drew himself up taller and threw out his chest, "I'll have you know, Guppy, that I'm in better shape than most of these younger fin-flappers. I been pushing the stragglers, and am in large part responsible for keeping this column together."

The Dohannen tended to store fat all over their bodies equally and I wasn't really able to tell just by looking who was fit and who wasn't. After months of living on stored rations, none of them were obese. But Krell, aged though he may be, was actually quite lean. I guessed that staying very fit was a holdover from his military days.

"Well, it's a good thing they have you," I told him. "Honestly, if we were moving any slower, I'd have doubts we'd make it before the Ravrath get their act together and come for us again."

"The military boys and girls are doing just fine, but the majority of civilians been sitting on their dorsals for the last few years. Hard to keep in shape when there's only one small workout room for over ten thousand people. But they'll make it, believe me. We're motivated to get the Frang out of here."

"Yeah, us too," I told him. "Believe me, this world is a paradise five hundred thousand years in the future. No Rav. Plenty of room to grow."

"Yes," he said, giving me the side-eye. "Be interesting to see how that goes. How your people intend to divvy things up. From what your Ensign Darkfeather told us, you're out here looking for colony worlds for your own species. Forgive an old man who's only dealt with his own politicians, but I can't help be a little... skeptical that we're not gonna get the belly fin to hang onto."

I translated that to 'short end of the stick' and shrugged. Realizing that he couldn't see my gesture through the Mark II, I opened my face plate and looked directly at him.

"Krell, humans are an admittedly young species, but," I gestured toward Kurakin and her squad, "we didn't come back in the past, putting our asses on the line to save your people because we're awful. The crew on my ship are, for the most part, the best and brightest of Earth's people. We are not going to leave you 'hanging on to the belly fin.'"

"I know you wouldn't young one, but you're not one of the leaders of your species. As far as I can tell, you're a mix of species and while I definitely feel you're sincere, you may not have any say in the matter."

He wasn't wrong. But I had more faith in Captain Yamashita, who'd most likely be the one negotiating agreements, than Krell had in his leaders.

"Well, I want to see how they manage it anyway, with or without my input. Any chance we can get these folks moving just a bit faster?"

"I'll see what I can do, Guppy, but my people evolved only bein' on land part time. We're just not as fast as you long-legged beasties." With that, Krell turned back toward the column and began consulting with one of the military women walking near us.

As we all moved toward the gate, I wondered about what the old Dohannen had said. I had every confidence that Captain Yamashita would do right by these people in the short term, though the logistics once we had them back on our side of the gate were going to be complicated. It was likely that she was going to send one of the Remoras back to Earth and get my father's people to mediate.

Once the Laldoralins were involved, all assumptions went right out the window.

"Security team, this is Dora. Our enemy has overcome their hesitancy and is now advancing in exceedingly large numbers behind you. I expect them to be within weapons range within the next fifteen minutes."

"Krell," I called out to the old Dohannen, "The Rav are on the move again. Time for everyone to give a last great effort."

"Now hear this," Krell bellowed out at his people. "We are so close, but the Rav can still get us, and feed us to that monstrosity beneath the waves out there. Everyone who has a weapon, move to the back of the column. Everyone that's unarmed move to the front. Then, you'll need to reach down into your depths and pull some more speed out. I know you're tired. I know your feet hurt, but this is the do or die moment. Once we're all squared away, start jogging to the gate. We're not far, you can do it and heal up later. Anyone falls, pull them up and push them onward! We need every one of you to rebuild our civilization, so leave no one behind."

"Dora," Kurakin said, "Distance to gate?

"One point two miles. You should have visual on it at this point."

I looked beyond the front of the column, and there across the plain I could see the gate. I switched to zoom mode on my HUD and watched as the last transport drove through the mirrored wall of the entrance. Even if everyone here on this side were wiped out now, we'd saved at least half the Dohannen and there was nothing the Ravrath could do about it.

The column had finished rearranging itself and the Dohannen picked up speed. We were close enough now that even they could see our destination. Fear and hope lent wings to their progress.

"Sec Ops team," Kurakin commed over our network, "Set all your remaining plasma grenades to proximity. If you walk over any depressions in the ground or see a spot that you can hide a grenade, leave a gift for our pursuers. They're already a little hesitant to ride into our meat grinder again. Let's give them extra incentive to slow down."

With the column moving faster, the gate seemed to be coming to us. However, it was only a matter of time before the least fit of the Dohannen began to lag. It didn't take that long for the orderly column of men and women to begin fraying around the edges and I could see people being pushed or helped along. When someone went down, Someone else yanked them to their feet.

"Mom? Distance?" I could see the gate ahead, so close buy yet so far.

"Point six seven miles. You are almost there, son."

"Voss!" Kurakin said. "Move on to the gate, be ready to help get these people through. Dora. Link me to Steranko and Jenkins. They've still got full load outs and we need all the firepower we can get."

I began sprinting toward the gate. As I ran, two Godzilla-suited team members passed me going the other way, toward the column. Watching them on my rear view screen, I saw them split at the head of the column one running down each side of it until they met with Kurakin's team at the rear of the column.

"Here they come," Kurakin's voice said. "Everyone pull in close. We'll form a shield wall for the column. Steranko, Jenkins, between you, you've got eight Stingers. Use them wisely for maximum disruption to the enemy ranks. Everyone else, use your remaining weapon power and munitions carefully. We want maximum return on investment."

I reached the gate just as the first plasma grenade mines began going off. I took up position on the opposite side of the gate from Ping. Looking behind her, I saw a generator exactly like the ones powering the gate on *Seeker's* end. Looking behind me, I saw its twin on the other side. Evidently, our people hadn't wanted to rely on a vulnerable power source miles away.

As I stood there, a Rav tank suddenly appeared from some nearby trees, and my heart went into my throat. It turned toward the column and sped off. I realized it was the enemy weapon we'd captured before, and Dora was sending it to defend the column. Hopefully, she'd inform Kurakin's people before it got there.

"Voss," Toravld said from beside Givall, who stood at the console. "Go through the portal. Make sure that everyone who's gone through to the other side is out of the way. We're about to have a huge cattle drive passing through in a few minutes and I need someone riding herd on the other side."

Explosions and weapons fire could be heard from the rear of the Dohannen column and looking back that way, I could see the landscape was black with Rav forces.

"Sir, our people back home are expecting to move big crowds through. They don't really need me to…"

"That was a direct order from your commander, Cadet." Ensign Ping Teo's voice was all business now. "So get your shiny metal ass through that portal! On the double."

I hated this. I'd been here from the start, I deserved to be there at the finish. But orders are orders.

I stepped through the shimmering wall of the gate.

Chapter Thirty

I stepped out of the portal expecting chaos. I wasn't disappointed.

Most of the previous group were out of the way and much father along the stretch of land the gate sat on. I could see crew from *Seeker* trying to help and herd them out of harm's way.

In front of me, what must've been the largest transport, sat about twenty feet ahead of the portal entrance. People were piling out and were walking away from the gate, with some being carried on stretchers. They weren't the problem. The problem was the vehicle itself. I knew when the second column of Dohannen came through, they'd probably be on the run and this behemoth was right in their pathway to create a logjam.

"Here I come to save the day," I said. I moved up among the Dohannen and *Seeker* personnel trying to push it and waved them aside. Then I set my shoulder to the rear of the transport and began pushing. The Mark II performed like a champ, and with one of the Dohannen driving, we got the offending vehicle a hundred feet to the side.

Commander M'Buku met me as I walked toward the portal. I also saw Emily Darkfeather running back toward us from where the Dohannen kept moving away from the portal.

"Cadet Voss," M'Buku said. "I need a sit-rep on what's going on over there."

"Sir!" I said, gesturing toward the mass of Dohannen that Emily had brought through. "Those people are just over half the population of Dohannen. The other half are in a moving column being harried by a large Ravrath force. Chief Kurakin and her team are coving their rear. Commander Torvald, Chief Moreland and Ensign Teo are at the gate with the scientist Givall. The leading edge of the column should start coming through any minute now."

"Commander," Emily said as she reached us, "we need to clear all non-essential personnel away from the gate. That includes *Seeker* crew except our security people and the technicians at the gate console there with Lalall. People are going to be in a panic and rushing to get through the portal."

"And we want to avoid a stampede and trampled Dohannen," M'Buku finished for her. "We should split the column three ways. Left side needs to vector thirty degrees left, right side thirty degrees right. Column center moves straight forward. Voss, get on it."

"Sir?"

"Time to play traffic robot, son. Get there in front of the portal, turn your speakers up and split that column up as they go through. Clear?"

"Aye aye, sir. I'm on it."

"Good man." M'Buku said. "Darkfeather, what is the status of the people we already have over here?"

I didn't catch Emily's reply as I moved toward the gate. I took up position ten yards out, and waited. I didn't have to wait long.

One moment the surface of the portal was a silvery-smooth mirror finish, the next it was filled with scrambling Dohannen. There were no orderly rows like ours when we'd gone to the past, just a mad scramble to get through. The way they were moving told me the situation on the other side was desperate.

"Everyone to the left side, move that way!" I yelled, my speakers making it impossible to not hear me. "Everyone to the right turn right and go that way!" I gestured to my right. "Everyone in the center, keep going toward me and continue on as fast as you can! We need more space for those following you. Keep moving as fast as possible without trampling each other."

The hesitation was only momentary, and then the swarm split semi-neatly. More Dohannen kept coming through, and the farther along the column we got, the more panicky they looked.

"Is anyone keeping a count?" I said to the technicians.

"Four hundred seventy eight so far in this group," he called back.

"Four seventy eight? This is going to take forever," I heard Emily say from the gate.

It certainly seemed that way. I stood, directing traffic for what seemed like eons as thousands of refugees passed me. Eventually I noticed that the rows of people coming through were starting to look less crowded. A few minutes later, Dohannen were coming through in threes and fours. Ping Teo, resplendent in her Mark II, stepped through between waves of people.

"Teo," Commander M'Buku bellowed over the din of the moving Dohannen, "I need a sit-rep! How many more? How much longer?

"Less than three hundred to go, Sir. The Chief and her team are at the gate, holding it. Torvald should be coming though any moment. There may be Ravrath on their heels when the last come through. Be ready." As she said it, the two Godzilla-suited security personnel that had stayed on this side moved closer to the edges of the gate.

Dohannen kept pouring through, then the flow stopped. A few moments later, the first of the Godzilla suits backed out of the portal, followed by another and then another. All of them looked pretty banged up and a few were smoking as they walked through. They lined up along the sides of gate, and I could recognize a forming kill-zone when I saw one.

Lastly, Commander Torvald limped through, followed by Givall and Chief Moreland. Seconds later, Chief Kurakin's terribly damaged suit moved through and it was obvious that she'd been providing cover for the two scientists and the chief.

"Lalall! Close the portal!" Givall yelled.

"Wait!" I cried out, "Dora's still over there!"

That moment of hesitation allowed six Ravrath to step through, another group emerging behind them. They'd barely stepped out, when a silvery streak flew out above their head, actually clipping a Rav soldier and sending him sprawling in the mud.

"I'm clear!" Dora said as she ascended up toward the sky. "Close it!"

The instruction was superfluous. Lalall had closed the gate the moment after Dora had flown through it. A row of six Rav soldiers had been stepping out of the portal, following the first six, as Lalall shut it down. The result wasn't pretty. Cleanly sliced off legs, arms and heads made it through to our side. The scene must've been equally horrendous on the other side of the portal.

The six Rav who'd made it through had backed together, weapons facing outward toward the Sec Ops team and their battle armor. Through their environmental suit faceplates, their eyes were wide. Their expressions, even with someone as alien as the Rav, seemed to be pure terror.

They weren't looking at our battle-armored team though.

After the gate had shut down, Dohannen had started filling the spaces between our people, with more of them coming up from behind. A low sound began from the crowd, not quite a roar but definitely a growl of some sort. The crowd was well past turning ugly, it was ready for carnage.

"People!" Chief Kurakin's voice rang out, "we need for you to step back and let us secure these prisoners. They will receive…"

Her words were too little, too late. The Dohannen surged forward like a tidal wave, many buffeting my suit to the point where my shields flared. Their fury was unstoppable and the Rav went under the first wave as if they'd been swallowed by a tsunami. I caught a glimpse of what was happening to the enemy soldiers, and turned my head away. I'd already seen enough horror to last me a lifetime. I didn't need a new set of nightmares to add to the ones I already was going to be living with.

There was nothing security could do either. To even attempt a rescue would've meant wading though a sea of our allies to protect soldiers of a genocidal regime. None of Kurakin's team even made the attempt.

◆

Later, I was out of my suit and standing with M'buku, Darkfeather, Torvald and Givall next to the gate at its console. I think we were all feeling a little ill at what had happened to the Rav who'd come through. My own reaction surprised me a little. I don't think I felt sympathy for them necessarily, but being torn apart by a mob wasn't any way any of us would've wanted to go.

Captain Yamashita had chosen the site well. It stood on a broad open plane, only a mile from the edge of the ocean on one side and a tectonic-collision-formed mountain range around sixty miles distant on the other. The crew of the *Seeker* would help to set up a temporary refugee camp. With our fabricators running at full capacity, it wouldn't take long to at least get shelters ready for everyone.

"Givall," M'Buku said, "Our captain has sent one of our probes back toward our homeworld to request a team from Laldora to help mediate what colonization rights that your people will be willing to grant to our people."

The Dohannen scientist looked surprised. "You recognize our claim to this world? I admit surprise. Your people could have returned here through the gate and left my people behind, yet you did everything possible to get as many of us to safety as you could. You'd be well within your power to shunt us off to a small island and claim Derilon as your own."

"That is not who we are," M'Buku replied. "While I don't doubt that there will be some on Earth who think we should do just that, humans as a species are trying to be better than our ancestors. I am sure that we can come up with an equitable solution for both our peoples."

"Derilon?" Emily whispered to me. "Captain Yamashita's gonna have to give up her naming rights to this world I'll bet."

She and I wandered away from the conversation. It was all way above our pay grade anyway. We'd noticed that many Dohannen had moved toward the ocean. It didn't take us long to walk there to see what was going on.

Everyone was lined up on the shore, looking at the water. There seemed to be a yearning in their expressions, and seeing Sikall right at the water's edge, I wandered down to her.

"Sikall. Hey there. Glad to see you made it okay!"

"Tanner. I'm happy you are here too," she replied. "I can't believe we are actually safe."

"Believe it," I said, pulling my padd off my belt. "Mom? You got your ears on?"

"My metaphorical ears are in fine function, son. What do you need?"

"We've probably changed history on this world. Any sign of the Rav?"

"I am still scanning Susanowo to find any major changes, and have taken the initiative to bring in the other remaining Remoras to aid me. Scans are no different that I can find, than when we originally surveyed the planet. The Ravrath do not exist in this time. Nor can I find any trace of the leviathan creature. My theory is that it did not survive the era of volcanic destruction on this world. If it is here, then even its bones are buried too deep to scan."

The padd, as it had been doing the entire time since she'd created the translation matrix, had simultaneously translated Dora's report. Sikall had been listening intently to our conversation. She turned to the crowd.

"Did you hear? Our friends have scanned the world since we came to this time. The Ravrath and the Kanemora are gone! Extinct! Pass it on!"

A murmur started moving through the throng of Dohannen, but soon grew into a raucous cheer. I was surprised when Sikall began to remove her clothing, stripping down naked and then waded out and dove under the water. Moments later, a horde of children joined her, frolicking along the edge and swimming for all they were worth. The adults followed in a mass, with clothing flying everywhere.

There was a big difference in how Dohannen enjoyed the water than if it'd been a group of humans. Rather than stay near the shore, as everyone would do in, for example Florida, Sikall and many of the adults swam far out, reveling in their return to what was their original environment. They were swimming much faster than any human could. I couldn't imagine how joyous that must feel, but the expressions on the nearer Dohannen gave me a glimpse of it. Emily and I stood watching them with big grins on our faces.

"Hey, Cadet," she said from beside me, "ever go skinny dipping?"

Chapter Thirty-One

A month later, the *LV Siranee*, a Laldoralin heavy cruiser, emerged from jump space far closer to the planet than a human crew would have returned to normal space. Lieutenant Fowler, who had helm duty on the *Seeker's* bridge at the time was heard to mutter, "Show offs."

Aboard were a Laldoralin diplomatic delegation and perhaps not surprisingly, an envoy from the Medegin. The Medegin wanted to meet these Dohannen that evidence pointed to being their ancestors.

By this time, in addition to helping the Dohannen fabricate and build shelters, Captain Yamashita had ordered a conference building created on the surface of the planet. The negotiations between humanity and the Dohannen could've been carried out in the spacious conference room onboard *Seeker*, but the captain had decided that might be intimidating for the Dohannen. Negotiations were conducted planet-side.

Attending were Captain Yamashita and commander M'Buku negotiating for Earth; Givall, Lalall, Dekell and Tivonne were there for the Dohannen.

The mediator was Jolanar, part of the same diplomatic team that had negotiated Earth's inclusion into the Laldoralin Galactic Hegemony over a century earlier. The long-lived elder race often mediated disputes between the younger races.

A surprise attendee was the Medegin envoy Kula. He had asked to be allowed to sit in on the proceedings, vaguely expressing a desire to keep an eye on his ancestor's interests.

Jolanar began the proceedings. "Greeting sentients. I have spoken with both parties in these negotiations and it is seldom that I have the pleasure of dealing with two groups who are, to use the human term, on the same page. But, if I may ask, Captain Yamashita, why are these junior officers here? I can recognize why you might want to have Krizon's offspring attend, (I felt my face turn red) but why the others?"

Captain Yamashita started to speak, but Tivonne interrupted.

"Esteemed mediator," she said, "these humans are here at the request of the Dohannen. I realize how irregular that might seem, but these... Commander Torvald, Dr. Carstairs, Ensign Teo, Chief Moreland, Ensign Darkfeather and young Cadet Voss, are the saviors of our people. Though many on the *E.S.S. Seeker's* crew aided us, put their lives on the line for us, this small group were the ones who engineered the plan that saved our remaining people. That brought us to this much saner time period. They are special to us. They are our heroes, and will be remembered in perpetuity."

My face wasn't the only one turning red now. Even Chief Moreland looked embarrassed.

Jolanar actually chuckled. The Laldoralin, my father's people, are a fairly unemotional lot. I guessed in the diplomatic corps, you needed to be a bit more animated,

"I see," he said. "Having been associated with the human species for some time now, I am not as surprised as you might think, Tivonne. They are a very young species and their two most dominant traits seem to be curiosity and inventiveness."

"Speaking of inventiveness," our captain said with a semi-smooth segue, "I have drafted a proposal for these negotiations. To summarize, though," A holographic representation of the world appeared above the table, "Derilon is segmented into three large vertical continents." (The captain's chosen name for the world had been superseded by its original Dohannen name) "I have highlighted a proposed territory for each race as you can see."

One continent glowed light green and had a small icon of a human, one was light purple and showed an icon of what could only be a Dohannen.

"Captain," Tivonne said, "I notice that the third continent seems unclaimed. What is your intention there?"

"That continent, which no one has named yet, should be this," She touched a control under the table. The unnamed continent began to swim with shades of green and purple, blending together. Human and Dohannen icons began appearing and populating the space. "I propose that this continent should be set up so that it is a conscious effort to blend our cultures. I want to avoid the sort of isolationism that can come when two different cultures coexist distances apart. I assure you, on old Earth, this caused more than a few serious problems, and we were all the same species."

"Intriguing," Givall said. "I can say with certainty that I endorse that idea. As long as we agree on certain guidelines to protect the planet, each faction could pretty much build their own civilizations. But this mixed-species area, that could be carefully planned and be an example to everyone of both species. I like this idea very much."

"We would be proud to share space with the humans," Dekell said.

"If I might interject," Kula, the Medegin envoy chimed in. "Mediga wishes to put forward a claim and an alternate proposal."

You could've heard a pin drop in the resulting silence.

"By what right does Mediga make a claim in these proceedings?" Captain Yamashita asked.

"By the unassailable fact that Derilon is the origin world of the Medegin, Captain. The Dohannen are our ancestors." He turned to Tivonne. "These humans you have such a high opinion of are children on the cosmic stage and a very junior member of the Laldoralin Hegemony. I have no doubt that you've seen the best of them in the crew of the *E.S.S. Seeker*, but I assure you these ones are an exception."

"Kula," Jolanar said, "your…"

"It might interest my Dohannen friends," Kula said, speaking over Jolanar, "to know that these beings had to be forceably prevented from destroying each other not so very long ago. Mediga, on the other hand, is a peaceful waterborne society with accumulated knowledge and technology thousands of years in advance of this child race. All of which we can share with you."

If humanity needed proof that we're not equal partners in the Laldoralin Hegemony, there it is, right in front of us.

"You could be our partners," Kula continued, "aside from being our ancestors, you bring something amazing to the table. Not only the ability for almost instantaneous travel, but the the ability to literally move through time."

I could see that Captain Yamashita, Tivonne and Jolanar all wanted to comment, but it was Givall who spoke first. He held up one of our handheld comms and spoke into it.

"Lalall my love, it is as I feared. Initiate the program." He said.

Moments later, Captain Yamashita's padd chimed with an incoming call. She answered it, looked concerned, and turned toward Givall.

"Yes Captain, I'm afraid that it's true," he said. "When your people first informed me of how they'd come to our time, I began working on a worm that was built into the calculations needed to make gate travel work. It is deleting itself across all systems. Even in the reports that you have sent to your home world, a time-delay worm will delete all information on the subject within a day. I assure you, it will harm nothing except the data regarding the gate."

"And the gate itself?" M'Buku asked.

"You will find that it has lost all molecular cohesion. The gate on this end is nothing more than the elements used in its construction. The gate in the past exploded rather spectacularly many millennia ago. The technology is gone and it only exists in my head now. While Commander Torvald may have a good understanding of what I created, I would ask him what the consequences might be to the universe if people began moving through and thus altering time."

"Unmitigated chaos," Torvald replied. "I will not reveal what I know, Givall, though I think you may be overestimating my understanding of the science. For example, I have no idea how to actually construct the gate."

"You… you have thrown this amazing technology away?" Kula said.

"The cost to the universe would be too high. It is gone," Givall said.

"Esteemed mediator," Tivonne said. "Is there any doubt as to whom the original, if you'll pardon the expression, owners of this world are?"

"There is none," Jolanar said. "Derilon is the homeworld of the Dohannen and as far as the Hegemony is concerned, they are sole owners. As much as the humans have done, any claim they have on this world would be at the forbearance of your people."

"The people of Earth recognize the Dohannen claim," Captain Yamashita said quietly. "If they do not want to share this world with us, or if they prefer to live with the Medegin, we will respect their wishes. *Seeker* is an explorer ship and we will leave to find new worlds to colonize and leave the Dohannen in peace."

"And this one calls you children," Tivonne said, looking coldly at Kula. "I need to discuss this with my colleagues. If you will excuse us." The Dohannen contingent left the room and walked away from the building.

I excused myself for a "bathroom break" and left also. I actually wanted to talk to Dora somewhere that the Laldoralin mediator couldn't hear us. Dora had left an iteration of herself back on my father's ship, but the version of herself with us was very unauthorized.

"Mom?"

"Yes Tanner, how can I help you, my son?"

"Givall deleted all information on the gates through a worm imbedded in the calculations. Are you okay?"

She was silent a moment. Then she gave what I could only describe as a digital sigh. "The information is also removed from my own systems. It is gone."

"But how? I mean your systems have to be centuries more advanced than anything the Dohannen have ever seen. How'd they get a worm into your programs?"

"Actually," she said. "They did not. Givall contacted me earlier and voiced his concerns. I agreed with them. I self purged the information myself a day ago."

"Phew, Mom," I said. "Please understand that I'm not saying you were wrong, but wow! That is a big decision that affects everyone who could've benefited from the gate travel tech."

"Yes, Tanner. It was. However, I agreed with its creator that it was too dangerous to be unleashed upon this reality. As they said in the old westerns that you watched as a child, 'I did what I had to do".

"Well, as far as I'm concerned, Givall's worm caught you off guard. That's my story and I'm stickin' to it. Probably best if it wasn't common knowledge that you deleted it on your own initiative. There are going to be some very sour grapes about this."

"On that we agree," she said.

I saw the Dohannen group walking back to the building. "Gotta go, Mom. Looks like the Dohannen may have made some sort of decision."

"Let's hope it's a favorable one, Tanner."

◆

We had all regained our seats when Tivonne stood up and signaled for quiet.

"Gentle sentients, we, the elected leaders of the Dohannen Remnant, have made a decision. Though there is much to be worked out, we would like to tentatively, with room for revision, accept Captain Yamashita's proposal. Perhaps two 'child' races can forge an alliance that even the elder races will one day envy."

"But, we are genetically related," Kula said, hands gesticulating wildly. "You barely have a viable population. Interweaving our species would make that a non-issue."

"We will welcome limited immigration from your world, Envoy. Strictly controlled, but your people will be welcomed. You simply will not be in control of this world's destiny. That is a fate that would befall the Dohannen, being under Medigan rule. With the humans, we can form a unilateral government that will serve all."

"But we can work something…"

Tivonne raised her hand to silence him. She turned toward the human delegation.

"Captain Yamashita. We, the elected leaders of the Dohannen do have a condition for this agreement."

"I would expect there would be many conditions, Madam speaker, but what is your specific concern?"

"Obviously, our people have come to this time and place with little more than what we could carry in trucks or on our backs. In other words, we are poor. What we want is help from our new partners in rebuilding an actual modern civilization and we're going to need all we can get. How soon before your governmental representatives can arrive so that we may begin swimming out the details?"

"As soon as you wish, "Yamashita assured her, "though travel both ways can take up to half a month. Otherwise, we are at your service."

"Then let the process begin!"

Chapter Thirty-Two

The delegation from Earth showed up around a month and a half later. They were accompanied by a small armada of freighters carrying supplies, materials and most importantly, large industrial fabricators. The forging of the Dohannen-Human alliance had begun.

E.S.S. Seeker had refilled all her supplies, made her repairs, and was soon to be on her way to our next possible colony system exploration. We'd also rotated out a few crew who'd had family emergencies back on Earth, as well as sending our one resident of the brig back to our homeworld for trial.

Dora had finally purged all of the native software from the *Beast*, and with a new operating system, it was given as a gift to the Dohannen for system defense. Dora removed her iteration from the weapons platform and reintegrated her selves back into Remora 2.

I was in my bunk, studying particle wave physics when the loudspeaker called out at the same time my padd chimed.

"Cadet Tanner Voss, report to the bridge immediately."

I jumped up, tugging on my uniform shirt and wondered what I'd done now. I hurried down the corridors, my room, of course, being about as far from the command bridge as you could get. When I finally reached the bridge, I realized something was up.

As well as the usual bridge crew and the captain and first officer, several other who wouldn't normally be there had showed up. Chiefs Moreland and Kurakin, Dr. Carstairs, Ensign Teo. Emily Darkfeather and Commander Torvald were regular bridge personnel, but I knew this was not their shift. They were there anyway. Something was definitely up.

"Cadet Voss," the captain said, "remove your cadet's jacket, please." I quickly did so. First Officer M'Buku handed her a dark gray and green bundle and I realized it was a standard officer's uniform jacket. My heart skipped a beat when she handed it to me and told me to put it on.

"Acting ensign, Tanner Voss. For service in the finest traditions of the Terran Exploratory Force, for actions above and beyond the call of duty you are promoted. You are now officially an officer of the *U.S.S Seeker*. Though you are at this point an 'acting' ensign, you will achieve the rank fully upon completion of your academy course work."

"I… I… thank you, Ma'am!" The captain smiled at me, and gestured toward the bridge.

"You've been doing well in your shifts on the secondary bridge and in your simulations. Chief Kurakin says you're ready. Ensign, take the helm. It's time for us to leave this world and continue our mission." Evidently, my improvements at piloting had been noticed.

"Aye, Captain!"

I stepped over to the helm, and Jim Fowler gave me his seat with a big grin on his face. I glanced over at Emily Darkfeather. She was beaming a huge smile at me and gave me a covert double thumbs up.

I sat at the helm station. "Helm is ready, Captain. Breaking planetary orbit on your command."

"Acknowledged. Take us out of here, Mr. Voss." A course appeared on one of my view screens, and I made the necessary changes. The view of the planet slid to one side and disappeared and we headed for deep space.

The *E.S.S. Seeker* moved ever onward toward our next adventure.

THE END.

Other books by Clint Hollingworth
Fiction
Voyages of the Seeker
Seeker One
Seeker Two

The Mac Crow Thrillers
The Sage Wind Blows Cold
Death in the High Lonesome
The Deep Blue Crush
Dying To Win

The Ghost Wind Chronicles
The Road Sharks

Non-Fiction
Wilderness Survival Knives: Tips for Choosing and Using
Wolves in Street Clothing (with Kris Wilder)

Graphic Novels
The Wandering Ones
The After Time
The Mad Scout
The Mission
The Road Home
Turf War
The Die Off (prequel)

Shin Kagé: Duel at the Derelict
The Timewalker

SEEKER ONE

In the tradition of the early Heinlein space stories, 1st in "Voyages of the Seeker" series.

Tanner Voss has an entire year left at the Terran Exploratory Force academy, so no one is more surprised than Tanner himself when he is pulled from the academy and placed on the Deep Space initiative as a cadet. For one thing, Tanner is still recovering from being in stasis for 150 years, with some odd and unexpected side effects.

These side effects might be what his commanders are interested in. Is Tanner being used for some purpose which will shorten his career abruptly, or does he have a future with the Deep Space Initiative? Are the DSI's enemies all on the outside, or are some on the ship?

Other NOVELS by Clint Hollingsworth

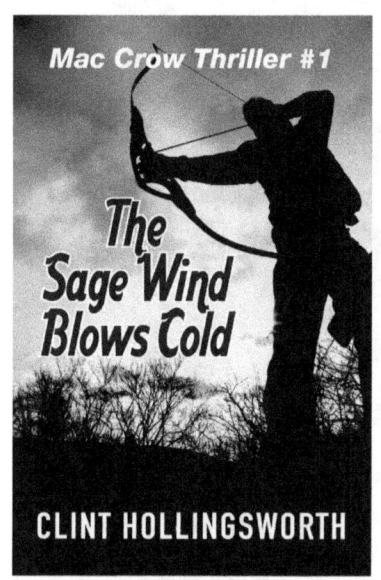

The Sage Wind Blows Cold

Deep in the woods, desperately following the trail, Mac comes upon an SAR volunteer face down in the forest with an arrow in his back. Little does MacKenzie Crow know, this is just the beginning of his problems.

Death in the High Lonesome

Mac and Rosa must escape from the deep mountains, with minimal gear during a blizzard, and to make things worse, they are being tracked by a killer who always seems to be three steps ahead of them. If Mac's skills of survival and tracking fail them, his and Rosa's bodies won't be found until spring time.

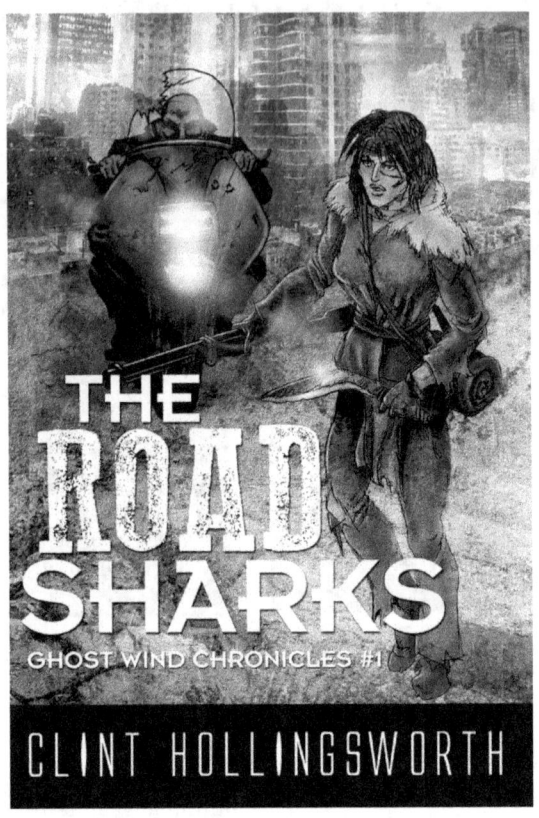

The Road Sharks (Ghost Wind Chronicles #1)

The story of Ravenwing's (The Wandering Ones) banished sister,
Ghost Wind.

In 2057, warrior scout Ghost Wind finds herself banished from
her people, cast adrift in a world ravaged by a man-made bio
plague. Looking for a new home, she meets Eli, the handsome rider
with many secrets, who hints at a place she might be welcome.
Unfortunately, she also meets the vicious fusion cycle gang,the
Road Sharks who do their best to make her life a living hell.

To survive, to have a new home, Ghost Wind realizes that she must
be just as ruthless as her enemies, and that standing on the sidelines
is a good way to lose everything.

The Wandering Ones

2066 A.D.-The Pacific Northwest. A man-made plague has wiped out 80% of the world's population, dividing the survivors into the Clan of the Hawk (following the way of ancient Apache scout warriors, Ninjas and Trackers); the Western Alliance, a technology based society; and the Neo-Nazi Farnham's Empire.

It's been thirty years since the great Die-Off. Ravenwing, master scout of the Clan of the Hawk must take in three untrained apprentices from the technological Western Alliance, and teach them how to survive in the brutal post apocalyptic world of 2066 a.d.